SIGNY CLAIMED

A WOLF SHIFTER FATED MATES REVERSE HAREM ROMANCE

BILLIONAIRE WOLVES SERIES
BOOK SIX

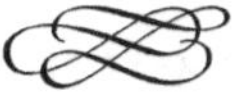

CHARMAINE LOUISE SHELTON

CONTENTS

WANT FREE BOOKS?

Want to know what happened to Jagger's best friend Dylan? Find out in *Dylan The Rogue: A Wolf Shifter Fated Mates Paranormal Romance* your FREE Book!

Click Cover Below or visit **bit.ly/ CLBooksDylanTheRogue** to subscribe to my newsletter for latest news and launches, books from my author friends, and sizzling reads in book promotions. Plus, start reading the steamy fated mates romance for bad boy wolf shifter Dylan.

FREE BOOK!

To read her current works, visit her Ream Stories account bit.ly/CharmaineLouiseBooksCoterie.

ABOUT SIGNY CLAIMED: A WOLF SHIFTER FATED MATES REVERSE HAREM ROMANCE

How far will my wolf shifter fated mates go to claim me? They'll burn down the world and take down anyone who stands in their way. Including me.

Garrett the grumpy leader whose glacial eyes pierce my soul.

Dolph the comforting beta whose musky masculine scent makes me shiver.

Colin the brute enforcer whose snark is as good as his bite.

They realize I'm their fated mate and want me as their queen of the New York Wolves Pack.

Before I recover my memory, I'm snatched from The Fortress. Now, their enemy holds me, and they will do anything to get me back. But what do I want, or does it matter?

*Their spicy reverse harem paranormal romance is part two of the standalone trilogy in the sizzling **Billionaire Wolves Series** of interconnecting stories featuring wolf shifter fated mates romance. Get a glimpse of their dynamism in other books.*

Anthem: "Through the Fire" Chaka Khan

https://www.youtube.com/watch?v=TjWmw-8-OEk

Visit CharmaineLouiseBooks.com

CHAPTER 1

olin

"Between all of you fuckers, you couldn't protect Signy?!" Viggo Larson shouts.

I step chest-to-chest to *Princess'*—rather Signy's older brother—and growl, "Fuck off! Do you think we'd let them take her? She's our fated mate!"

As silence descends around the chaos within Alpha Garrett Moen's office at The Fortress, in my mind's eye, my wolf swivels his massive tawny head in my direction. If a wolf could have a questioning expression on its face, his eyes would pop and jaw drop at my admission.

Yeah. Signy Larson—only moments ago known as *Princess* to Garrett, Dolph Pihl, and me—is our fated mate.

Our, as in all three of us. Our mate destined by the gods. Three wolf shifter males to one she-wolf. For us to claim and to live happily fucking ever after forever.

The idea of such a pairing—well, grouping, I suppose—is rare in wolf shifter packs. Most have two in the relationship, be they fated mates or not.

And it's damn sure foreign to me, the pup whose mother abandoned him and his father. A father who then turned bitter and ranted about the worthlessness and pain caused by mates to an impressionable pup. He certainly didn't fail to ingrain the dislike of a mate on my young mind. Which hasn't changed. Until now. Thanks to *Princess.*

The she-wolf whose private jet crashed near to The Fortress in Greene County, New York. The thousand-plus-acre mountain location serves as the training and survival facility for our enforcers and is a place to interrogate enemies. An imposing stone structure with a surrounding wall straight from Viking times. Authentically erected by our ancestors millennia ago.

Scandinavian Viking wolf shifters sailed from the Old World and landed along the East Coast of what's now the United States. The six packs headed by best friends who sought new lands moved throughout the continent to form territories, with ours settling south of here. Moen Island off East Hampton became our base, and we're now known as the New York Wolves Pack. The other packs govern Los Angeles, Sedona, Las Vegas, Aspen, and New

York. We maintain close ties with our brethren through friendship, mating, and business. Plus, our Ruling Council gatherings keep us informed of happenings throughout the packs.

Along with her name, we learned Signy is the pack princess of the Miami Wolves Pack. The crash did more than kill the other four wolf shifters aboard. A head injury erased Signy's memory. She knew nothing of herself or of being a she-wolf.

But what Garrett and Dolph knew from the moment we found her amongst the wreckage is she's their fated mate. Naturally, Mr. Anti Mate didn't recognize the signs until my best friends spelled it out for me. But I recognized her unique scent of the forest after a spring rain, woody and earthy, with a hint of wild honey straight from the comb. The scent all three of us inhaled as our first breath when we were born imprinted on our brains.

But that wasn't enough to override years of never wanting a mate, fated or otherwise. Yet here I am all up in her brother's face. Snarling. Fangs bared. Chest expanded. Hands fisted as claws prick my palms.

His ice blue eyes, so like Signy's, flash silver with his wolf close to the surface too. He returns my snarls and doesn't back down. His anger and frustration at losing contact with his younger sister for weeks proves palpable.

If I could step back and see the situation from his perspective, I would give in. But that's not me. I'm the alphahole of the three of us. I back down for. No. One. Not even for *Princess.*

My gut churns as I recall the many snarky comments I made as I rebuked the intoxicating draw of my connection to her.

"I don't want anything to do with you, anyway. So, I'll take my 'freak of nature' ass to the dungeons. I have more important shit to do than to listen to a whining, no-memory-having she-wolf."

"No-go, Princess. I'm not your boy toy Dolph."

"Hold on, Princess. I still don't want a mate."

And here I am, wanting her as my mate. Dumbass. I didn't see what was right before me. Now, she's gone and in the hands of a fiend—Raulf Blaise. I thought my worse nightmare was having a mate. No. It's said mate held captive by a sick as all fuck breeder and his gang. Who knows who she is and will use her to get back at us.

No wonder Garrett didn't want a mate, either. Although his reasons were for what's happening—her in the vengeful hands of his enemy. I can tell by Garrett's actions he regrets not claiming her, too.

Only Dolph knew and gave in to his instinct to acknowledge his fated mate. He refuses to give her up. I can also tell he'd challenge any male who laid claim to her prior to our presence in her life. Despite Garrett insisting she make the choice to stay with us, both he and Dolph reconsider his command. I sure as hell do.

Princess is ours. I will allow no one to keep us apart, including her overprotective brothers.

I glare at Viggo and snarl.

"What the fuck did he just say? Fated mate? *Our?*"

My attention turns to Jagger as the room temperature drops to an Arctic level. Fists curled at his sides, the formidable Alpha glares at Garrett. He spits blood on the stone floor before he can speak.

"Yes. Dolph, Colin, and mine. Signy is our fated mate."

Viggo curses and spins away from me. Her brother paces the floor with clenched fists.

Jagger's molars grind loud enough to be heard over his brother.

Dylan and the pack doctor narrow their eyes on us.

"Listen, Jagger and Dylan, you know what it is to know your fated mate. I don't know about you two," Garrett says as he looks between Viggo and the pack doctor. They nod. "The only difference is Signy has three—"

"I don't think so, Moen," Jagger growls. He raises his hand when the three of us protest and continues. "But I don't have time to get into it with you now. We have to find my sister. Tell me what happened."

Since the blizzard stopped, we prepared to depart for Moen Island. The three of us managing the enforcers to clear the roads and helipad, repair the communications tower, and to confer with the team remaining. We left Signy in the infirmary where she was last seen by the nurse. At some point, Signy left. Walked right out of The Fortress and off the road.

In wolf form, the three of us detected the scent of unknown male wolf shifters blended with hers and followed it to a clearing. Disturbed snow leading to the center, and no further tracks confirmed a helicopter hovered above and took off with her and the males. To fuck knows where.

Instinct told us Blaise was behind it. Who else would dare to intrude upon The Fortress? We have his tech guru. Or rather, had since Garrett ripped his beating heart from his chest when he wouldn't divulge information on Blaise's location.

Now, we only have the encrypted email and video to go on. Thankfully, Thyra—Garrett's younger sister—is a tech wiz and will have info for us soon.

But not soon enough as I listen to Garrett fill Jagger in up to the last time anyone saw *Princess*, being the nurse in the infirmary. Garrett hesitates before he goes into who took her. Jagger growls low in his chest. The fucker's body bulks up even more. Garrett, whose no slouch, grips the back of his neck and squeezes. He defers to the other male out of respect Signy is his sister. Then continues glancing at Dylan, who works with us on the breeder missions since they captured his fated mate prior to their meeting and after. I watch him, knowing the MMA fighter will not react well to Signy being taken by another ring.

"Dylan, you know the missions we do—"

"Fuck. No." He growls as his sizable hands fist at his sides. He turns to Jagger. "Fucking breeders."

All the air gets sucked out of the office.

Jagger turns flashing silver eyes on Garrett, then Dolph and me, and growls.

"Pray the gods are on your side because if I do not get my baby sister back, I. Will. End. You. All."

Despite his anger being well placed, as we are at fault for not watching her more closely, I bristle at his threat. My wolf, who also doesn't appreciate his tone, snarls and snaps his teeth. With my eyes flashing golden, I step to the Miami Wolves Pack Alpha.

"The fuck you mean, you will end us? You think we want *our* fated mate in the hands of that nut job?" I growl and continue when he narrows his silvery gaze on me with lip curled. "Hell no! So, if anybody is pissed, it's Garrett, Dolph, and me—"

"Enough!"

"Back down!"

Dolph and Rust step between us.

"We don't have time for flexing. Signy is our focus—for all of us. Got it?"

Dolph pins us with his gaze until we nod in agreement.

He's right. No time to waste.

DOLPH

. . .

I CAN'T SAY I blame Signy's brothers and her pack for being surprised she was taken under our watch—former Army Special Forces trained for protection and combat.

We followed our fathers and theirs before them to West Point and in our roles in the pack—Garrett Alpha, me beta, and Colin head enforcer. We graduated from the United States Military Academy with the rank of Second Lieutenant and rose to Commanding Officer for Garrett and First Lieutenant for Colin and me.

As Green Berets, the three of us became guerrilla warfare experts and use unconventional tactics to fight terrorists abroad. No longer on active duty—although we're called in for special missions—we focus those skills to dismantle the racket. That is when we're not running Moen, Inc.—Garrett's family's multibillion-dollar arms and aircraft manufacturing company based in New York City. Thanks to it, we have the latest weapons and transportation for our missions. Ones we'll use to fight for Signy's release.

I would have laughed had someone told me my fated mate would drop from the sky, then get snatched back up by a deranged maniac.

Now, I fear for what he may subject her to by his hands, causing my heart to race and stutter in my chest. Hands, I plan to chop off with my machete and shove them up his ass.

However, I don't have time to fantasize about his slow and painful death. It's time for action and no more posturing by the males in this room.

"Enough!" I shout as Rust, the other pack's doctor, yells for Colin and Signy's brother to back down. I glare at everyone in the room, including both Alphas.

"This pissing match stops now," I say into the ensuing silence. "Facts, Signy is our fated mate; they took her without our knowledge; a sick fucker has her; we act. Now."

"I agree," Garrett says. Blue fire rages in his glacial eyes.

"So do I," Jagger states as he stares at Viggo. They appear to communicate telepathically as an Alpha can with his pack, similar to the connection shared by mates.

Unfortunately, neither works over great distances. Otherwise—despite not having issued the claiming bite—we would have been able to speak internally with Signy. The bite would have also embedded a serum with our scents beneath her skin, marking her as ours permanently. No other male wolf shifter would dare to touch her. Although it wouldn't keep the likes of Blaise from taking her if given the chance.

I rub a hand over the center of my chest to ease the ache in my heart. It began a different beat when I first detected her scent amongst the fumes from the private jet's wreckage. The feeling intensified over these last few weeks, especially after the intimate acts we shared. The closeness increased our connection.

We wanted to give her time to regain her memory. Now, I wish we weren't so honorable and claimed her fully. Had we done so, I doubt she'd be anywhere but by our sides.

"Now that we're on the same page, all kumbaya and like, let's get our asses in gear already!"

Colin's growl jostles me from my musings.

He pins each of us with a piercing glare, then stomps from the office.

Garrett glances at me, and we nod.

"Right. Give me a second to dress, and we'll roll out," he says, gesturing at the cargo pants that ripped during a semi-shift when he saw the video of Signy with Blaise.

A video of her only covered by a sheet spread-eagle with her wrists and ankles handcuffed to an old iron bed. Him kneeling between her thighs licking blood from her busted lip as he grins at the camera. His hand around her throat keeps her facing the camera. She stares at it wide-eyed as tears slip down her pale cheeks. Tousled hair frames her face.

It was enough to make all three of us lose control, with me ranting and Colin shifting into his wolf fully. My vision tinges red from the memory of her stricken face and her exposed body. A body we should experience intimately, just us three.

I give my head a mind-clearing shake. Time to step up as pack beta while Garrett changes.

"Okay, let's head to the helipad."

I gesture for the males to follow in Colin's wake through the door. With faces set in determination, they turn and march out. I nod at Garrett as he steps into a new pair of cargo pants, then I stride after them.

Moments later, I settle next to Garrett with Colin across the aisle aboard one of our pack's helicopters. Jagger sits beside Rust while Dylan sits across from them. Viggo hunches in a back row, glaring out the window.

They rode with us instead of on the other helicopter. It's best for us to strategize and to share communication should Thyra contact Garrett in-flight.

The air is thick with tension as Jagger watches the video. He insisted, despite Garrett's recommendation he not put the sordid images in his mind. But her eldest brother ignored him. Viggo refused, as did the others.

Anger rolls over Jagger's features until he closes the laptop and his eyes. After a deep breath, he faces us.

"I will be the one to kill this motherfucker. My face will be the last he sees before I send him to *Hel*."

Garrett nods slowly.

"Agreed. However, first, we will torture the fucker for information on the rest of the rings. We will save Signy and any she-wolves, turned human females, and pups at the location. But we must rescue the others too. He must have knowledge that can help us."

"Fine," Jagger concedes.

And like Viggo, I turn and stare out the window, silently urging the pilot to fly faster.

We don't know how much time remains to save our fated mate.

But what we do know is we'll burn down the world and take down anyone who stands in our way.

CHAPTER 2

 *igny*

I'M scooped from the chair. Dolph carries me to a table and lays me out like a platter. Wordlessly, he and Garrett remove my clothes. Dolph tugs the boots and drops them to the floor while Garrett grips the hem of my Henley. Still knotted, it drags up my torso as I rise with arms extended overhead. My breasts tumble free. They growl in unison, then latch onto beaded nipples.

They furl tighter in their warm, wet mouths. Tongues wrap around the sensitive tips and suckle. Teeth nibble and scrape. My back arches as my fingernails scour the wooden surface, seeking purchase behind me.

Hands unbuckle my belt, and my pants rip open as they feast on my breasts. Garrett trails open-mouthed kisses from my breast, along my flank, and down my hip as he lowers the pants. He tosses them over his shoulder and grabs my ankles, yanking me to the edge of the table. Our gazes connect. His feral. Mine wanton.

He licks his lips and lowers his mouth to my throbbing pussy. I cum just from the swipe of his tongue from my puckered hole, over my dripping folds to my swollen clit. A garble cry pours from my mouth as my entire body convulses. He growls and laps as the juices flow from my quivering pussy.

Another growl sounds behind me.

My head whips in its direction.

Dolph squats stroking his ginormous cock. The tip weeps. He smirks as I lick my lips. Grabbing a fist full of my hair in his other hand, he pulls me flat on the table. My head tilts back to a glorious, up-close view. I only have seconds to admire it before he flips around and kneels on either side of my arms. His cock bobs above my face. My eyes fly to his. The smirk widens as he taps his tip against my bottom lip.

My mouth falls open of its own accord.

As he presses it into my willing mouth, Garrett's tongue spears into my pussy. I moan around Dolph's girth. Both men groan in satisfaction.

Garrett licks, bites, and kisses my pussy as he devours

it, grunting during his feast. My hips circle, grinding on his face. Fingers join in, probing my inner walls. One strokes my G-spot, and I keen arcing from the table.

Dolph has none of it.

He fists his cock, sliding it back into my slack mouth. I watch him with hooded eyes as my lips wrap around the slick, bulbous head. My tongue slides along the underside, pressing his cock to the roof of my mouth. I inhale through my nose, sucking him deeper. His girth still makes me gag. Fingernails dig into his muscular thighs. He withdraws slowly, dragging his cock along my tongue.

"Breathe, Baby Girl, and swallow me down your throat. I want to see it stretched by my dick."

I shiver at his dirty words. But eagerly comply to please him. My throat relaxes as I breathe. He slides deeper, a golden gaze locked on where his cock disappears between my lips. The salty taste of his pre-cum makes my mouth water for more. As I inhale, his musky scent fills me. I need more.

One hand cups his sac and massages his heavy balls while the other hand grips his ass, pulling him closer. His head drops back with a guttural growl. My lips kiss his groin. I hum pleased with myself.

"Fuck, Baby Girl. You take my cock so well," he rasps as his fingers trace the outline of his cock in my throat. His cock twitches, and he groans. "So. Fucking. Good."

Each word punctuated with a rotation of his narrow

hips as his hand tightens its hold on my hair. My scalp tingles.

But not as much as my pussy.

Garrett kneels behind Dolph. Electric blue eyes stare at me from over his shoulder. His lips and chin shine, coated with my pussy juices. He lifts my legs straight up and rests them against his chest. They're wedged between him and Dolph's back.

"You are delicious, Princess. But I want to feel you cum from my cock," Garrett growls.

I feel the thickness of his cock as he rubs it along my soaked seam. I mewl around Dolph's cock. He pulls out and taps my lips as I moan wantonly from Garrett's long, slow strokes. My legs tremble.

He increases his pace, and Dolph slides his dick back into my mouth. They find a rhythm as they seek their release. My cheeks hallow out as Dolph's cock grows impossibly larger. He holds my head still and pistons his hips. His eyes bore into mine as his cock pulsates. Hot ropes of cum shoot straight to my belly. I add more suction to milk him of every drop.

Garrett's fingers dig into my inner thighs as his dick surges against my slippery folds. The wet sounds mingle with his grunts and growls. He lifts my hips from the table, changing the angle. His tip hits my clit with each stroke.

"Get ready to cum with me, Princess," he grinds out through clenched teeth. The tendons in his neck stand out as he strains to match his release with my orgasm. "Cum. Cum for me. Now!"

Dolph's still hard cock falls from my mouth. My fingernails dig crescents into his forearms. The back of my head bangs against the table as the orgasm zings down from my crown and up from my toes to detonate within my core. I wail as Garrett roars with one final thrust.

Copious amounts of his cum jettison from his cock to spray my belly and my breasts.

"Fuck that's hot. The Alpha has marked you," Dolph growls as he smears the creamy jizz into my skin, already wet with sweat.

Garrett collapses forward, bracing his hands on either side of Dolph's knees. His forehead rests on his shoulder. Labored breathing mingles with my whimpers.

I close my eyes as aftershocks rip through me. My empty pussy contracts. My legs lower as Garrett climbs from the table. He stands beside me and scoops some of his seed onto his finger. I watch as he brings the fingers to my mouth. I open it on a moan. Silently, he feeds it to me. His cobalt blue eyes don't waver from my mouth. My tongue laps at his digits until they're clean.

"Such a good girl, Princess," he murmurs in a raspy voice as he cups my cheek.

I mewl at his praise and close my eyes, pressing into his palm.

Wake up.

The demand filters through the lust-filled fog of my

memory. Languorously, my heavy eyelids drift open. Heat flushes my sweat-dampened skin. It buzzes with electricity from the phantom caresses of my lovers. My vision clears.

Then reality crashes over me, dousing the passionate fire racing through every cell of my being. I guess my mind wanted to provide a respite from this horrible situation.

Trapped.

In my mind's eye, my ebony black wolf paces. The white patch on her back bristles. Her gray eyes flash silver as her gaze bores into mine. A growl pours from her mouth as she bares her sharp teeth.

Wake up.

Fully aware, I tug at the handcuffs, anchoring my wrists and ankles to the corners of the iron bed's headboard and footboard. The metal chafes my flesh, even as it heals from previous attempts to dislodge the handcuffs. But I can move only so much, or risk displacing the thin cotton sheet and reveal my naked body.

The gods know I have no wish to expose myself further to the male wolf shifter captors. Bile rises in the back of my throat at the thought of their lecherous stares, or gods forbid, their salacious touches.

During the helicopter ride, their reference to *breeding* and their ramped desire to return to their base baffled me. When they jogged to the large barn, I assumed they intended to give into their beastly sides and fuck animals. But no.

Now, their Alpha made it clear their intention is to breed me. I suspect they keep other she-wolves in the barn rather than livestock. They're like the men who captured Sasha Volkov, now Vang, since she mated Dylan after he saved her. With Garrett's help. These must be the secretive missions he, Dolph, and Colin go on and want to protect me from.

Sasha never speaks of what happened other than to say they never touched her sexually. But she witnessed other she-wolves and turned human females forced to have sex with their captors. Then the females crying when the wolf shifters took their pups from them at birth to be sold. Sasha endured physical and mental abuse. Thank the gods she's better now, and they saved the others with her.

In a similar position, I understand the horror they experienced and why Garrett won't claim me. He knows his enemies will use me to get at him. And this Alpha proves Garrett's concern valid.

The memory of being in his and Dolph's arms return and with it my heart clenches remembering Colin doesn't want me—not just to keep me safe like Garrett. But because Colin dislikes me. What must he think now that the males took me? Does he regret the mean comments he made? Or does he feel the connection for me as I do for him?

Regardless, Garrett and Dolph want me and will find a way to save me.

And what must Jagger, Viggo, and our parents think? They must be losing their minds with worry. No communication from me in weeks. The pack must be in an uproar. Without a doubt, my family will do all they can to find me.

With a bit of hope simmering in my heart, I glance around the room, hoping to find a means of escape. Torn curtains hang at a window. Faded floral wallpaper peels from the walls. A closed wooden door is opposite me. Nothing of use appears in my limited range of view.

The room is as dilapidated as the rest of the old farmhouse and large barn. I noticed the disrepair when two male wolf shifters hauled me from the helicopter. The property sits in a field surrounded by trees. Snow blankets the area, not as deep as around The Fortress. But enough to cover the ground and the forest. The last rays of the sun painted the sky gold, red, and blue as it dipped behind mountains in the distance.

The beauty of the surrounding area contrasts with the state of the farmhouse. More gray siding than white paint remains on the exterior. A few windows lack shutters, and those with them hang askew. The roof lacks shingles and slopes in places. A broken swing rests below a window. The porch steps sagged and groaned as we crossed to the front door that squeaked as it opened. Inside, more monstrous males hang about. Their hungry gazes fixed on me.

I shuddered then and shudder now. My wolf howls mournfully. Only the threat of being shot with silver bullets to the knees prevents me from setting her free and fighting for our freedom.

Truly a scary house, and I'm trapped in a hellish nightmare.

arrett

"I GET THE URGENCY. But you fogging up my monitors as you hover too close behind me does not help, you know. Give me some space to work here, G. Gods."

I barely control an eye roll at my younger sister, who doesn't move her gaze from the four monitors on her desk. She jabs a quick elbow into my gut without stopping her fingers from flying across the keyboard. I grunt and step back.

"Thank you," she snarks as she tosses her waist-length hair over one shoulder. Its vibrant purple color matches the fitted t-shirt she wears with equally tight black jeans and platform Doc Martens. As usual, her curvaceous body is on display. "When we get Signy back, you can breathe all over her, not on me. Okay?"

"Thyra, behave," our father Arne growls. "Less talking and more typing."

She mumbles a response lower than our enhanced hearing can detect.

I cast our father a glance of gratitude. He nods and folds his arms across his powerful chest.

Although no longer pack Alpha, all members respect him as a former leader. As do many past Alphas and Lunas, he and our mother Idonea travel extensively to visit other retired leaders around the world. Fortunately, they returned from their most recent trip abroad before the blizzard. In my and my beta Dolph's absence, my father stepped in. For which I'm grateful, since he kept Jagger and his pack from losing their shit.

I shift my gaze to the Miami Wolves Pack Alpha. His intense gaze remains locked on the monitors. Viggo stands beside him with his hands shoved into the pockets of his jeans. He must sense my gaze and flicks his eyes in my direction. I offer a tight smile. He ignores it and returns his gaze to the monitors.

Dolph and Colin stand behind me on the other end of Thyra's desk. Dylan and Rust sit with their elbows pressed into their thighs on guest chairs behind us. They too watch as she works on the encrypted email with the video file.

As I swing my gaze back to the monitors, my mother

saunters into the office, followed by my younger brother Randel and a couple of pack members. They carry trays of sandwiches, snacks, and beverages. My stomach rumbles at the scent of the giant pastrami and melted Swiss cheese on rye from Katz's Deli on East Houston Street in lower Manhattan.

"Hello sweetheart, I figured you may be hungry and your favorite sandwich would tempt you to eat," she says, then glances around the room. "And that goes for all of you young males. We brought plenty for you to eat. You can't save Signy if you don't have any energy and your brains are bleary."

Murmurs of thank you, Luna, fill the room.

"Soon, our New York Wolves Pack will have a new Luna—"

Low growls from Jagger and Viggo interrupt her. She arches an elegant eyebrow and pins them with a sharp stare.

"Hush your grumbling, Jagger Larson and Viggo Larson," she says, with all the authority of a powerful Luna. "I know for a fact your mother, Sigrid, would not appreciate you meddling in your sister's future with her fated mates. You may be Alpha, Jagger. But I remember when you were born and just a pup. Am I clear?"

"Yes, Luna," Jagger and Viggo say in unison as their cheeks deepen in color.

I hide a smirk behind a bite of my sandwich but catch

the eye of Dolph, who doesn't bother to hide his amusement at their chastisement.

"Thank you for your support, Luna," he says with a respectful nod.

My mother purses her lips and turns her gaze to him.

"Don't gloat, Dolph Pihl. You, Colin, and Garrett should have kept your Luna close to you. I don't blame her brothers and pack for having less faith in you as her fated mates. You better make this right."

She looks at each of us, then sweeps from the room with the pack mates behind her. Randel stays behind.

Silence descends on the room. Furtive glances pass amongst us. Each caught in their thoughts until the booming laughter of my father displaces the tension. We turn to him with eyebrows raised. He shakes his head as his brown eyes twinkle.

"And that's why Idonea ruled this pack by my side. She's a force to reckon with, one you want on your side," he says with a chuckle. Then the mirth leaves his face.

"And she's correct. We cherish and protect she-wolves above all. The three of you better find Signy and destroy every last one of those sons of bitches. I've been in contact with the Ruling Council. The other four packs are on standby to support New York and Miami. Too many of them have missing she-wolves and suspicious reports of human females who disappeared. This goes deeper than your previous missions. Handle it, Garrett."

"Yes, sir," I respond, taken back to his rank as Major above my Captain.

He nods.

"I will leave you to it. I have calls to make, including one to your father, Jagger and Viggo. Just as Idonea is close to your mother, Marcus and I share a history beyond being Alphas. Contact me with any developments."

We watch as he strides from the room.

"Your father is right—"

"We need to work as allies—"

Jagger and I speak at the same time, then nod in agreement without having to finish our sentences.

Signy outranks all.

"Well, that's fine and dandy. Now, will you leave my office so I can work in peace?"

We chuckle at Thyra, who doesn't bother to glance our way as she speaks. Her eyes remain on the monitors and her fingers fly.

"Fine. But let me know as—"

"Yeah, yeah, yeah. I got it. Byeee!"

We troop out and head to my office suite down the hall of the building. We use it for pack meetings and as Moen, Inc. offices on the island when we're not at our headquarters in Manhattan. For the next few hours, we hold video conference calls with the other pack Alphas and strategize. Mutual determination replaces the tension as we set aside egos and work as a focused unit.

Despite preferring to keep at it, we agree to regroup in the morning unless Thyra discovers Blaise's location before.

I invite Jagger and the guys to stay on Moen Island in one of the guest houses. After they realized Signy was missing, they tracked the last location of her private jet with coordinates, placing it in upstate. They couldn't find anything in the area through their research and couldn't reach me for information. Instead, my father told them the jet landed near The Fortress. They flew up to Moen Island over a week ago. But the blizzard kept them from reaching us further north. My father gave permission for them to stay at a hotel in Manhattan.

Having them here is twofold. One, they're close should we need to fly out immediately. Two, Dolph, Colin, and I need to bridge the chasm between us as Signy's fated mates and her brothers. Not that we need their permission. The gods know we will make Signy ours, no matter who we piss off. However, I don't want her loyalty pulled in two opposing directions. She's ours and their sister. We can coexist. Plus, packs must remain harmonious for the survival of us all, especially when facing threats like Blaise and the other breeding rings.

Jagger must agree to set aside our pissing match since he readily accepts my invitation. I arrange for a couple of pack members to pick up their luggage once the maids pack the bags up. Then we head for the dining hall.

"Moen Island reminds me of our Moon Island, except with snow," Jagger says as we ride along the main road. "I don't understand how the hell you deal with the cold so many months of the year. Blizzards? Bah! Give me balmy Biscayne Bay over the chilly northern Atlantic Ocean any day."

I chuckle as I glance out the SUV's window and see Moen Island from a visitor's viewpoint.

Set off the coast of East Hampton, Long Island between Moen Bay and the Atlantic Ocean, our pack's island gets the brunt of cold weather during the winter. Even the spring and summer seasons are cooler out on the water. But the island's natural beauty makes up for the inclement weather.

Moen Island spans over nine miles long and five miles wide with five-thousand-plus acres of old growth forest and over thirty miles of coastline, including pristine beaches. Aside from the building used for our pack meetings and for Moen, Inc. offices, other structures, and mansions, along with our private airstrip and marina, dot the island. A village with our hospital, school, shops, restaurants, hair salon, barbershop, spa, grocery store, and library afford us a place to use when we prefer to remain on the island and not venture to the mainland. The ultimate in privacy.

I'll take it over any other place in the world, no matter the weather.

My mind drifts to Signy and what she'll think of Moen Island as it will be her new home, despite her brothers' protests. I will not allow my mind to think she won't be here. The gods wouldn't tease us with our fated mate, only to never claim her as ours.

I give my head a quick shake to clear it of any negative thoughts.

We'll get her settled on Moen Island—in my mansion. Dolph and Colin have theirs on either side of mine. They can visit or spend the night. But Signy will be in my bed, even if I have to pull rank as pack Alpha and thus, she's our Luna.

My wolf rumbles in approval as his glacial blue eyes focus on mine. We're in full agreement.

Perhaps I'll give in and get a bigger bed for the four of us to share. I'm not so selfish.

However, if Signy needs a place to call her own, she can take over one of my guest suites as her private retreat. And if she doesn't like the rest of my mansion, she can redecorate it. In fact, I'm sure Dolph and Colin will let her put her touch on their houses, too. Anything to make her more comfortable and to acclimate to her—*our*—new life.

That extends to the rest of her life. Whatever she needs, we will provide—a new wardrobe, laptop and mobile, a car and driver. Signy will want for nothing.

Just as crucial is her reconnecting with her wolf. Had she shifted, she may have gotten away from Blaise. Once she's home, I will not let her go a day without calling forth her wolf. She will learn to protect herself again. Plus, we'll run with the pack around the island in the dense forest where no outsiders can spy on us. Allow nature to take over.

And just as I don't give a damn what her brothers think, the pack will have no choice but to accept our foursome. It may be unusual, but not unheard of. They'll welcome her as our fated mate, as the gods decided on our match.

We have the support of my father and my mother and Dolph's parents—Birger and Revna—will stand by us. Colin's father? Questionable since his mate left him when Colin was a pup and Brandt turned bitter. Sadly, I'm sure his father's rants shaped Colin's belief in mates, fated or otherwise. Although his current behavior shows he's accepted Signy as ours.

As have I. I will no longer allow my fear of losing her to one of our enemies to keep us apart. Now that one has her, I realize just how much she needs to be in my life.

There's more to what I do. Moen, Inc. Life on Moen Island. I'll spoil her with all my billions can buy.

But first, we'll claim Signy and complete the mate bonding ceremony. Proclaim her as ours before all since we'll invite her pack and the others. It will be a huge affair where she will walk to us at the ceremony bower. Her eyes bright with love. Our future written all over her face.

Her father will hand her to us without hesitation. And Jagger and Viggo will not interfere.

As the SUV stops in front of the dining hall, I turn from the window to face Jagger and cock an eyebrow.

"I don't give a damn whether you like Moen Island. Only Signy's love for her new home and for her fated mates matters."

CHAPTER 4

"DAMN, *princesse,* you have this room smelling like a barnyard. Perhaps we should have put you with the other breeding stock in a barn stall."

"Yeah. I thought the princess only had a pea in her bed, not that she *peed* on her bed."

The raucous laughter of the alpha Blaise and his flunky beta Bernard bounces off the walls of the bedroom. It increases as humiliation burns my cheeks.

My eyes close as I try to distance myself from their lewd comments as they continue. The cold puddle beneath me a reminder my bladder couldn't hold on any longer. Too many hours cuffed to the bed with no means of avoiding wetting myself and the mattress.

The acidic urine mingles with perspiration and fear. The stench floats in the air. Our heightened sense of smell easily detects the unpleasant odor. I chose to ignore it as best I could. These two harp on it hoping to degrade me further. It works.

I don't want to wallow in self-pity. However, I can't help but to wallow in the puddle. My chest expands and drops on a pathetic sigh. My wolf stares at me with baleful eyes.

Why? Why did this have to happen to me? First, a plane crash kills my pack members. Then I lose my memory. The brief upside of my time with Garrett, Dolph, hell, even Colin, snatched away as Blaise's men yanked me from the safety of The Fortress.

But I can't give up. I must remain strong and pray to the gods the three of them will find me. I know Jagger and my family must be searching for me. They know I was bound for New York and the jet crashed north of the city. It must have a black box or something to account for its whereabouts. Gods! Let them get me away from these monsters. I beg you—

"Don't you dare lie there and ignore me, *princesse!*"

My ears ring as stars dance in the darkness behind my closed eyes. I cry out from the slap upside my head as my neck jerks. The impact strong enough to disable a human jars me to the point of tears. I cry out in surprise.

Rank, hot breath skitters across my cheek.

"Listen to me when I speak to you. You are not too good for me, *princesse.* You will respect me. Open. Your. Eyes. Now."

My eyelids blink several times to focus my vision. Tears trail down to pool in my ears still ringing from the blow. I grit my teeth to bite back another cry. I will not give him the satisfaction of witnessing the pain he inflicted. Fuck. Him.

My gaze slides sideways to his face, inches from mine.

His beady eyes glow with his wolf near the surface. He curls the corner of his lip to reveal an elongated fang. The crude threat does nothing to me. I will remain strong despite the situation.

"Better," he snarls.

Garlic.

I swallow the bile that rises in my throat as my empty stomach roils from his foul breath. But I don't close my eyes. My head turns to maintain direct eye contact. He's not my alpha. And I will never submit to him.

"You're filthy. I refuse to fuck you in this condition," he says, then rises and grips the bulge at his crotch. His tongue dips from his mouth to lick his puffy lips. "Even if you have my cock hard as granite."

Bernard guffaws and says something in French.

I ignore him. Instead, my focus remains on Blaise. My gaze dart back from his hand to his face. Heat floods my face. Monster.

He joins in the laughter. Lust-filled eyes drag from my face, over my naked torso, still covered by the thin white sheet, and down to my bare legs. He grunts and nods his head. They exchange comments in their native language as they continue to ogle me.

"But don't you worry, *princesse*. Estrid will clean you up and get you ready for me in no time," Blaise says, then leans close to my face. "Then it will be you and me for weeks. I won't stop fucking you until I know my pup grows in your belly."

Despite my bravado, my eyes close and a sob escapes as my entire body shudders.

"Aw, don't worry, *princesse*. Soon you'll cry my name as you writhe beneath me, taking my cock like a good girl."

Pain shoots through my breasts. My eyes pop open with a yelp.

He grins down at me like the devil himself as his thumbs and index fingers pinch and twist my nipples through the sheet. He winks and strides from the room. Bernard follows him but pauses at the door. He smirks at me, then jerks his chin up with a kiss.

The door closes behind them.

I sag into the mattress and let the tears flow freely. My wolf whines softly.

Moments later, the door squeaks open. I turn my head in the opposite direction, not wanting to face the male wolf shifters again. I can take but so much.

The door closes. Footsteps too light to be either big

man approach the bed. It must be Estrid. My cleaner. I pray to the gods she won't torment me further. They must hear my prayer as a hand rests on my shoulder. The gentle touch draws my gaze towards her.

An older she-wolf close in age to my mother, Sigrid, stands beside me. Amber eyes scan my face, pausing at what must be a fresh bruise on my cheek, then lower over my body. No malice fills them, only concern. She returns her gaze to mine and offers a small smile.

"Hello, I'm Estrid. Do not be frightened. I'm here to clean you up—"

"And prep me to be bred!"

She flinches at my outburst. Her amber eyes lower as she sucks in a breath and shakes her head.

"I am sorry. Truly. But there's nothing that can be done. Consider yourself fortunate you are in the main house and not with the others in the barn. Alpha Blaise has made it clear you are his. The others are not so lucky. Any male can have them whenever and however they choose."

Estrid pauses and lifts her slight shoulders with a resigned sigh. Despair etches lines in her gaunt face. She flattens her lips and pats my shoulder.

"I want to help you as much as I can," she says and pauses until I raise my eyes back to her face. "You and the bed are soiled. Let me clean both, make you as comfortable as I can, given the circumstances. Will you let me?"

My eyes flutter closed as the enormity of my situation falls heavily on me. As much as I may pray and hope for rescue, the present is the present. I am trapped by a ring of breeders. No one can save me at this moment.

Tears burn the backs of my eyes. Sobs rack my chest. Never in my life did I think I would lose my virginity to a monster. My dreams of being with my fated mate, or rather now, mates, will end in moments. Gods help me.

"Come, now, child. Know you are alive and the gods will give you strength to endure whatever Alpha Blaise puts you through. You won't like it, nor want it. But you will survive. I will help you as much as I can, just as I do with the others. Okay?"

She rubs my arm. Her fingers touch the handcuff.

I stiffen as my eyes snap open.

She shakes her head.

"Don't. You won't get far. There's a massive wolf shifter right outside the door and another one stationed below the window. You don't want to anger Alpha Blaise. Trust me."

She mutters the last part as a click fills the air, and the handcuff slips from my wrist. She rubs the reddened and torn skin with a salve as I consider her words.

She's right. I won't get away. Resigned, I wait as she frees my limbs from the wretched handcuffs and applies more salve. My stiff muscles protest as I sit up and swing my legs over the edge of the bed. The odor rises from the still damp mattress. I gag and drape the sheet around my body.

Estrid works in silence as she removes the soiled bedding. She carries it to the door and swaps it for other linens in a basket. She glances at me and nods her head towards a closed door on the opposite wall.

"That's the bathroom. Wait inside while they switch out the mattress."

I don't hesitate and hurry to the door. Male voices fill the bedroom as they work. I glance around the bathroom. A filthy sink and tub with no shower curtain and a toilet with no lid are what I have to use. My heart fills with more despair. How far I've fallen.

Ignoring the grime, I turn on the water for the shower, let the sheet fall to the floor, and step beneath the stream. Goosebumps rise on my skin from the cold water. Despite wolf shifters having a higher temperature, I shudder as I look for soap. Nothing.

A knock on the bathroom door catches my attention.

My hackles rise.

Blaise? Already?

Then I shake my head.

That monster would never deign to knock. He'd barge right on in. It must be Estrid. I call for her to enter.

She passes a bar of soap and a bottle of shampoo to me, then places a threadbare towel on the sink before she leaves the bathroom. The masculine scent of leather and tobacco leads me to believe the toiletries are for a man. Why would Blaise allow the *breeding stock* access to beauty products? Again, I shake my head and sigh. The bastard.

Clean and dry, wrapped in the damp towel, I take a deep, cleansing breath before I turn the doorknob to face my fate.

Relief washes over me when I see only Estrid in the bedroom. She hovers by the footboard. Fingers twine in the tattered black cardigan she wears over a black dress paired with worn sneakers. The light from the overhead bare bulb glints on the gray streaks in her tawny hair, pulled back in a severe bun.

She smiles kindly.

"I know the water is cold. But I hope you feel a bit better, child."

I swallow back a retort, knowing it's not her fault, and she's only trying to help me as best as she can. Instead, I shrug. The bed draws my attention, even though I'd rather look anywhere but to the spot of my imminent defilement.

She must sense my anger and shakes her head.

"Remember what I said. You do not want to upset him. He will hurt you enough to inflict terrible pain. But he will still continue to use you for his benefit," she says and stares at me until I nod. "I brought you some food. Eat. Keep up your strength, child. He will be here soon."

The bile I held at bay rises like a geyser. I spin on my

heel and rush to the bathroom, barely making it to the toilet. My stomach heaves as I drop to my knees and bow my head in the ceramic bowl. My eyes close as tears slip down my cheeks.

Gods help me.

CHAPTER 5

olin

"Listen, I don't want trouble between our packs. But you have to understand where Jagger and I are coming from."

I side-eye Viggo as we sit at the head table in the dining hall. This male here. What makes him think I give a shit about where he and his brother are *coming from*? I don't. My only concern and focus are on Signy. Getting my *Princess* away from those bastards, ending them, and Garett, Dolph, and I claiming her as ours. Forever. That's it.

I tip the crystal snifter to my lips and sip the aged Macallan. The single malt whisky glides over my palate. Its oak, butterscotch, apricot, and cranberry flavor notes dance along my tongue before the smooth amber liquid slides down my throat. I wish it were Signy's sweet taste bursting across my tastebuds as I eat out her pussy like a starved male.

"Signy is our younger sister. It's our responsibility to protect and provide for her. Then she disappears. We're unable to contact her, locate her private jet, but can't get to her. When we finally reach The Fortress, a fucking lunatic has kidnapped her."

"How the *hell* do you think we feel? *Her fated mates?*"

I don't hold back my snarl. This male needs to understand where Garrett, Dolph, and I are coming from. She's ours now. Our responsibility. No one else's.

Viggo's growl vibrates from his massive chest. He sits taller and glares at me with the same ice blue eyes as Signy. Fuck, I miss her.

I flick my hand as though swatting away a gnat. My lip curls in disgust.

"Leave it, Larson. I will not tolerate more of your bull-shit. I have enough on my mind without having to listen to you bellyache."

He opens his mouth for a retort. But I cut him off as I stand.

"I don't want trouble between our packs either. But the gods help you if you keep pushing my patience. Do you understand where *I'm* coming from?"

I glare at him, then pivot on my boot heel, not bothering to wait for his response. I need some fucking air.

Dolph calls to me. But I wave him off without breaking my stride. If I don't get out of here, I'll blow this place up. And then we'll have even more problems. Problems I don't need interfering with plans to rescue our mate.

I pass pack members sitting at other tables. I feel the intensity of their stares as I march for the double doors.

Garrett made the announcement about Signy, her being our fated mate, her capture, and our rescue plan before dinner. They were shocked—about the foursome and the kidnapping. However, they were unanimous about getting her back at all costs. The vocal support of his and Dolph's parents helped to ease concerns about the unusual mating situation.

Naturally, my father Brandt's face filled with disgust. He can't get past my mother abandoning us when I was younger. She turned her back on him as a mate and on me as her pup. I can't say that I blame his bitterness or the leeriness he put in my head about mates. She hurt us deeply.

And Signy paid the price as I behaved poorly towards her. Now, I regret my actions.

I run a hand across the back of my neck and squeeze. The muscles stiff beneath my palm. My head drops and rolls from side to side to loosen them, to no avail. I'm wound up and need a release. I push the doors open harder than necessary and burst forward into the entry.

"Hey there, Colin."

I skid to a stop and turn at the seductive voice I know so well.

Patricia.

The she-wolf and I fuck occasionally, nothing serious. If the need arises, we take care of it. Simple. Wolf shifters think nothing of nudity or casual sex, unlike humans and their hang-ups.

But unlike other times, my cock doesn't throb at the sound of her voice or the sight of her lush curves. Nope. Nada. Zilch. Nothing stirs below my webbed belt.

Further proof Signy is the one for me.

My cock twitches at the mere mention of her name. Pissed I didn't partake of her bounty when Garrett and Dolph feasted on her after our get-to-know-you dinner at The Fortress. Like a fool, I stormed from the dining hall and left them to enjoy one another. Meanwhile, I jerked off outside the closed doors as I listened to their pleasure. I drag a hand over my face with a sigh.

A dainty palm on my forearm jolts me from the memory. I lower my hand to find Patricia smiling up at me. The tip of her tongue darts out to moisten her full lower lip.

Ordinarily, my cock would jump at the chance to bury itself in the wet warmth of her mouth. But again, nothing. Not a damn reaction.

Good.

I know who I want. And it's not this she-wolf in front of me. It's my *Princess* trapped with a maniac. Who the gods only know what the fuck he's doing to her, not to mention the fuckers with him.

A growl rips from behind my clenched teeth as my chest expands, my canines elongate, and my fingernails extend into claws. I curl my hands into fists as I partially shift in anger.

"Colin!"

Patricia's shocked cry brings me back to the room. Visions of Signy being harmed linger as my wolf throws his massive head back and howls. I shake my head to clear it and refocus on the she-wolf in front of me.

"Apologies, Patricia. I need some air. Excuse me," I growl in an inhuman voice as I jog for the exit. I leave her calling my name.

Once outside, I increase my pace to an all-out run. I grab the back of my turtleneck sweater and yank it over my head, tossing it to the side. My claws rip at the belt and zipper of my cargo pants. They shred into ribbons and flutter to the ground. I only pause long enough to pull my combat boots off.

A bestial roar splits the air. It reverberates around the dimly light road.

My vision reddens as my wolf surges to the forefront. The sensations of my bones reshaping and muscles lengthening to shift me from my human form to that of my great tawny wolf block out all else. Crackling and a flash find me on all four massive paws within moments. Ignoring Patricia's cries to stop, my beast runs for the woods. He bounds along the road, off the side, and lands on the grass before racing to the center of the island.

A perk of our private island provides a safe place for members of the pack to run in wolf form unencumbered. We run as a full pack a few times a month. The vast expanse and relative safety offer an ideal setting for our numbers.

Now, the island's thick forest calls to me. I need to outrun the pain in my chest and the frustration in my mind. My fated mate is not with us, snatched from us by others. In another male's arms. A feral howl pours from my throat.

I run past trees and bushes covered by snow. The scents of hibernating animals fill my nose. But don't mask the unique scent of Signy. I can never forget it. The forest after a spring rain, woody and earthy with a hint of wild honey straight from the comb. With a snort, I dash between some evergreens. Snow drops on my thick tawny fur.

Glimpses of other pack members in wolf form appear amongst the foliage. Not wanting to interact, I increase my speed and head towards the other end of Moen Island. I run for what seems hours. A normal wolf would have tired by then, muscles strained to capacity. As a wolf shifter, my body heals quickly unless silver is involved. Then it can be fatal.

I drag my weary body to my mansion and shift. As I do, the scents of Garrett and Dolph drift to me from the living room. My best friends rise from leather chairs. Dolph holds a t-shirt and a pair of joggers in his hand. Concern fills their faces. Unfortunately, the pain in my heart doesn't abate as I put on the clothes.

I run my fingers through my disheveled hair and drop onto the leather sofa across from them and stare into the roaring fireplace. Garrett hands a tumbler filled with amber liquid to me. I toss more Macallan whisky back in one gulp, then refill it from the decanter on the table. Downing that one, I pour another and lean forward with my elbows on my thighs and my head hanging. I twirl the tumbler and watch the orange and reds of the fire as prisms in the crystal.

They sip their whisky in silence, giving me the time I need.

"Here's to not wanting a fated mate to having her, then a maniac kidnaps her," I say as I raise my glass in a mock toast. "What an absolute shit show."

Garrett cocks his head and pins me with an intense stare.

"You do realize we will do all we can to get Signy back, right?"

"We will kill those fuckers and bring her home. Then make her ours forever."

"But what if we're too late?"

We eye each other, then lapse into silence. Only the snapping of the logs in the hearth fills the living room.

Where the hell are you, Signy?

CHAPTER 6

igny

"Oh, child. I'm so sorry you have to go through this. I truly wish I could do more to help you."

Estrid kneels beside me, rubbing circles on my back as I sit on my heels in front of the toilet bowl.

"When he's with you, let your mind go to a place and time where you're happiest. Hold on to that solace, no matter what happens. Let it carry you away from the moment at hand. If he allows me, I will come to you afterwards and…"

Her voice catches. She takes a deep breath and continues.

"Take care of you. Comfort you as much as I can. Now, just breathe, child. Just breath."

My stomach clenches, ready to heave up whatever acids remain. My body rejects the thought of Blaise's sleazy hands on me. There must be a way out of here. Think, Signy!

"Come now. You need to put something in your stomach to ease the nausea," Estrid says as she grasps my shoulders and rises, bringing us both to our feet. For an older, frail she-wolf, she still has strength in her.

I let her lead me to the bed and sit me on its edge. She places a bowl of stew and a spoon in my hands. Her nod of encouragement spurs me to eat a spoonful. Ordinarily, the savory flavors of the venison, potatoes, carrots, and green beans in a hearty broth would pique my appetite. Sadly, I fight not to retch.

She pats my shoulder and hands me a thick slab of bread.

"Eat what you can. But remember, you need your strength."

I nod and manage a few more bites. The bread helps to bind the stew in my stomach. The queasiness subsides. My mind wanders to memories of playing with Jagger and Viggo out in the Everglades, swimming in the Atlantic on South Beach with other she-wolves from our pack, and binge-watching Bridgerton with my mother while my father rolls his eyes.

Instead of bringing me a respite, tears prick at the backs of my eyes. I sniff and swallow another bite of the stew. Estrid is right. I need my strength. Because somehow, some way, I will get away from this horrible place and find a way to save the others, especially Estrid. Her kindness deserves to be rewarded.

I glance at her and offer a wan smile.

It drops from my face at the banging of the bedroom door against the wall. Paint chips flutter to the hardwood floor.

We gasp and jump to our feet. I nearly drop the bowl but manage to set it on the tray by the bed. My eyes never leave Blaise's face as he looms in the doorway. Bernard peers at me from over his shoulder. Both of their eyes narrow as they flick between me, Estrid, and the food.

"What do we have here? A tea party?" Blaise growls as he stomps into the bedroom. A voice rises from the walkie-talkie at his hip. He snarls and raises it to his ear. "I said, 'I will be at the helicopter shortly!'"

He slams the walkie-talkie back into its holster and stops in front of me. A devilish grin spreads across his face.

Estrid remains frozen in fear. In defiance, I raise my chin and hold his gaze.

"Unfortunately, duty calls. I must leave you, *princesse*. But when I return, I will put my pup in your belly."

He grabs the back of my neck with a beefy hand and

hauls me to him. Our bodies collide as he slams his mouth to mine. His broad tongue presses past my lips, slack in shock. He rolls his tongue around, prodding at every inch of my mouth. The stew and bread churn in my stomach. He lets me go just as the undigested food creeps up my throat. I gag it back down as I plop onto the bed, a hand raised to my mouth.

"Delicious," he smirks. "I can't wait to savor your sweet pussy."

He pivots on his boot heel and strides from the bedroom. With a wink, Bernard closes the door behind them.

I jump from the bed and rush to the bathroom. The water in the spigot isn't enough to wash away the garlicky taste of Blaise. I clutch the sink with a white-knuckle grip and hang my head that beats like a bass drum. I take a deep breath. Thank the gods I have more time to avoid that monster.

But when he returns?

I choke back a sob.

Be strong, Signy!

A hand on my back comforts me.

"Come, child. You need to get some rest."

Once again, Estrid leads me to the bed. This time, I sink onto the mattress and let her cover me with a fresh sheet. Along with the now dry towel, the sheet adds another layer of protection for me. My heavy eyelids flutter closed as the stress of the situation hits me hard and the drop in adrenaline wears off.

"Sleep, child."

My eyes fly open as Estrid steps from the bed. My hand shoots out to grab her arm. She turns in surprise.

"Please. Please stay with me. I—I don't want to be alone. Please."

Her eyes fill with sympathy as she nods. I slide over and pat the bed. She hesitates, then nods again as she lies down beside me. Her body stiffens when I rest my head on her shoulder. Then she relaxes and strokes my hair.

If I close my eyes, I can pretend as though I'm at home in my bed with my mother holding me close. A happy place I can lose myself in.

"Let me tell you about myself. I feel it's important for someone to know who I am in case… in case something happens to me. I want my family and my mates to know what happened to me. Is that all right?"

Estrid nods and listens as I tell her about being the Miami Wolves Pack Princess, the crash, my memory loss, and my fated mates. When I mention the New York Wolves Pack, her breath hitches. Her reaction makes me curious to learn who she is.

"Estrid, if you don't mind, would you tell me how you came to be here?"

I can't imagine Blaise uses her for breeding at her age. And she seems too nice to be a relative of his. Besides, she doesn't have the French accent he and Bernard speak English with. Who can she be?

"Twenty years ago, I traveled for a spa day and dinner in Manhattan. I told my mate I needed a break, a chance to unwind. Alone. I was always putting him and our pup ahead of me. He had his life as the head of the pack's enforcers while I was at home raising our pup. Sure, I had the rest of the members to spend time with. But I was young and wanted to experience life more. You know how packs shelter their she-wolves. Being a stay-at-home mother with only her mate and pup to care for wasn't enough for me. Resentment made me lash out at him.

"As the enforcer, he put his work protecting the pack first. A mate was secondary. It wasn't until he established himself as a formidable force did, he seek a mate. Still attractive and sexy. Many she-wolves wanted him. They knew him for his skills beyond fighting and strategy. A virile male."

A smile quirks the corners of her lips.

"Ours wasn't a fated mate pairing. He was fifteen years older than me. So, when he focused his attention on me— a much younger virgin—I was smitten. It was a whirlwind courtship. After a few weeks, we had our mate bonding ceremony. Shortly thereafter, I conceived—ever so fertile. Over the years, my infatuation with my mate waned. He was still very active with the enforcers, and I devoted myself to caring for his needs and raising our pup. Small things irked me—him coming home late, less sex, not another pup. I needed a break."

She pauses as though gathering her thoughts.

If she traveled to Manhattan, she must be a member of the New York Wolves Pack.

Wolf shifters—especially she-wolves along with pups are the most protected members—remain within their territories. Not that another pack would do them harm. But one would need permission from the pack's Alpha to enter their territory. Rogue wolves can upset the dynamism of an established pack.

My curiosity pushes the tiredness from my body as I sit up and look at her. She lifts her body and presses her back against the headboard. Her thin arms wrap around her knees as she draws them to her chest. Her gaze fixes on the opposite wall.

"After a day of beauty treatments, I was more than ready to enjoy a fancy restaurant, have drinks at the bar, followed by a nice dinner. Well, a male sat beside me at the bar. The hairs on the back of my neck rose when I detected the scent of an unfamiliar wolf shifter. His wolf flashed in his eyes as he grinned at me. I fled the restaurant."

She shudders and tightens her grip around her knees.

"I reached the sidewalk and hailed a cab. Before one could stop, a hand gripped my waist. I turned to look up and felt the prick of a needle in my neck. All went dark."

I gasp as tears shimmer in her amber eyes.

"I awoke naked in a dog crate in the back of a truck filled with other females in cages, including humans. All of us were terrified and wailing. Escape was impossible. And they maimed or killed those who tried. My will to survive kept me from following others in their attempts at freedom. For the next fifteen years, I gave birth to many pups and never saw mine or my mate again. Night after night, I whispered goodnight to my mate and pup, pretending to hold them in my arms, then cried myself to sleep. I never had a chance to tell them I'm sorry for being so selfish. My biggest regret in life."

A wistful expression fills her face as she shakes her head.

"My captors exchanged me many times, and I moved from one location to the next around the country. We never stayed long in one place. Five years ago, I ended up with Alpha Blaise. I bore one last pup before my body failed to produce more."

Tears slip silently down her cheeks as she continues.

"He was going to kill me as they do with the she-wolves and turned human females who can no longer give them what they need. They could never let us go for fear of someone learning about them. I begged him to let me live. I explained I could care for the others, keep them in line, healthy. I would rather stay alive and help the others than to die and leave them to face these *males* alone. My maternal instinct drives me to care for them. Blaise agreed."

She turns to me with a watery smile.

"And it's a good thing. Otherwise, I would never have met my daughter-in-law."

I gasp.

My wide eyes search her face for any resemblance to Garrett, Dolph, or—

"Colin is my pup."

arrett

"SITTING around like this drives me crazy. We need to do something! Not sit on our asses all day. Blaise must have left some sort of trail. What the hell is Thyra doing?"

After two days, even the calm Dolph loses patience. Like a caged feral wolf, he stomps along the hallway outside of Thyra's office. His buzzed golden hair stands on end. Stubble covers his normally clean-shaven face. A face now creased by a frown—eyebrows dipped, eyes narrow, nostrils flared, mouth tense. Flashing topaz eyes glare at Thyra's door on his umpteenth pass.

"Fuck!" He growls and swipes a large hand over his face.

I glance at Colin.

He leans against the wall opposite Thyra's door. Body coiled, ready to spring forth. His hooded amber eyes remain fixed on it as though willing her to open the door and announce she's found Signy. He remains silent while Dolph rants.

Movement in my periphery brings my attention to Jagger and Viggo. The brothers converse in low tones with their heads close. Shoulders hunched and legs rigid. I can't decipher their words. But their body language lets me know tension runs high in them too. Jagger must sense my stare. His ice blue eyes flick to me. He quirks an eyebrow, then shakes his head when I offer nothing. Viggo doesn't bother to glance my way.

Dylan and Rust appear at the end of the hallway. They stride over on long, muscular legs. Their eyes scan us gathered in the hallway before settling on their pack mates. As they pass me, Dylan jerks his chin in acknowledgement, Rust nods. Cold air from the outdoors wafts off them. A chill runs down my spine. I watch them as they reach Jagger and Viggo. Their whispers join the brothers' private conversation.

We may commit to work together to find Signy. But they make it clear as glass they don't trust us to take care of her. Can I blame them? No.

Dolph, Colin, and I take full responsibility for letting her out of our sight. We should have known Blaise would retaliate at the first opportunity. Instead of focusing on preparations to leave The Fortress and allowing Signy to roam around by herself, we should have demanded she remain in the infirmary. They never would have captured her if she were within the fortified walls of The Fortress.

Anger rolls through me—at myself.

As the pack Alpha and the Commanding Officer on our missions, I should have maintained better control of the situation. Remained on guard at all times, as I always do. But this time, my head was in the wrong space. The singular goal took precedence: get our fated mate home to Moen Island as soon as possible once the weather permitted.

Now she's gone, and we're no closer to finding her than we were days ago.

Dammit!

The need to do something rides me hard. I storm to Thyra's door and bang on it with my fist. Naturally, she locked it to keep us *out of my hair while I work to fix your fuck-up*. Three more bangs, and the door flies open. Her glacial blue eyes flash electric with her wolf as she glares at me.

"What. The. Absolute. Fuck."

Her gaze scorches a trail from my eyes to my feet and back.

"Do not *dare* to bang on my door, Garrett Moen!" She folds her arms over her breasts and pops a hip. She doesn't move to let me in. "I told you a million times, I will let you know when I find something. I get you're upset."

She pokes her head out to eye the others who gathered around me once she opened the door.

"All of you. And I'm sorry Signy is missing and in danger. I am working nonstop to find her. You're not helping me by hanging about"—she brings her gaze back to me—"or by knocking my door down like the big bad wolf. Go! Go spar or workout to let off some steam. And. Leave. Me. Alone."

She steps back and slams the door in my face. The click of the lock's tumblers emphasizes her command.

Dammit!

"I have to say, Thyra is right. I'm going for a run in wolf form. If anything pops off, howl. I won't go far from here," Jagger says.

"I'll join you," Rust says at the same time as Dolph. They nod at one another and follow Jagger down the hallway.

A jab to my flank has me spinning around with a roundhouse kick.

Dylan guffaws as he jumps back with the grace of a trained fighter.

"You need to stay on point, my friend. Let's spar in that fancy gym you have," he says as he slaps a sizable hand on my shoulder.

"Good idea," Colin says as he eyes Viggo. "You need a lesson, too."

Viggo throws his head back and laughs.

"Don't let my pretty boy looks fool you. Bring it, tough guy."

We troop out of the building and head for the state-of-the-art fitness center next door. We reach the glass doors, and I open them. With a sweep of my hand, I gesture for the others to enter ahead of me.

Immediately, the grunts and growls of wolf shifters—male and female—lifting weights, sparring, and doing calisthenics reach our ears. The scent of sweat and blood overpowers the cool air of the outdoors. Bright lights illuminate the interior. I step inside, and the doors shut automatically.

A glance around the vast space reveals areas for free weights and weight training machines, rows of treadmills, rowers, and climbers, heavy and speed bags, and fighting mats and rings. Sections for stretching and mats for exercises round out the space. Doors to the locker rooms with steam rooms, saunas, ice baths, and showers accessed at the furthest corners of the space.

Randel kicks a heavy bag held in place by another male. I call his name for him to join us, then exchange greetings with pack members working out. They appreciate seeing their Alpha sweating right alongside them. The camaraderie keeps our pack tight. My younger brother catches up to me as I head to the locker room to change.

"Any news on Signy?" He asks.

"Not yet. Thyra kicked us out."

He chuckles and shakes his head.

"You know Thyra, especially when she's on to something. Best to let her do her thing," he says with a grin. Then his expression sobers. "But don't worry. We'll get your mate back and end those fuckers. They'll never hurt another she-wolf or human female again."

I clap him on the back.

"Thanks, brother."

The guys and I change into shorts provided for the gym. We gather at the fighting mats. I place my mobile outside the border.

Dylan grins.

"Ready for your lesson, G.?"

"You mean, are you ready for me to hand you your ass, *D.*?"

The MMA fighter cracks his neck as he bounces on the balls of his feet.

"Bring it," he says as he punches his fists together.

The others fade away as Dylan and I face off. We circle one another around the mat, gauging weaknesses and chances for an opening strike.

"Come on, pussy boy. Show me what you got," Dylan taunts with a smirk.

I won't let him bait me. Instead, I set aside all other thoughts and go into fight mode. Strategy and skill take over. The need to win flows through me.

Dylan sees a chance and takes it. He delivers a round-house kick to my left flank.

Damn… that shit hurts like a motherfucker.

"And they call you Captain. Bah—"

Whack!

"Not so captainy now, huh—"

Bam Bam!

"Now, I'm beating your weak ass like a pussy—"

Before Dylan's next series of blows can hit me, I quickly crouch low and use my leg to sweep him off his feet. The giant wolf shifter lands on his ass with an oomph.

"What were you saying, asshole?" I sneer as I circle him, cracking my neck from side to side.

"Not bad. What else you got for me?"

Dylan punches his fists together as he effortlessly backflips to land on his feet.

"Oh, that and a whole lot more, D."

I fake a charge at him, then at the last second turn and back kick him, the momentum throwing him off balance and causing him to stumble forward. I follow the kick with a few well-placed punches, then taunt him as I float backwards, fists in the air, "What were you saying?"

The sparring with Dylan goes on for another hour. The MMA fighter is in top form from his underground fights and training. But I'm no slouch. Green Beret training and my Alpha genetics make me a daunting opponent. We end the session evenly.

"Not bad. Although you need to work on your front kicks," I taunt. "Definitely room for improvement."

"Yeah, right. Tell that to your busted lip," he responds with a snort. "We better find Signy soon, or else I'll have you unrecognizable."

His reference to Signy missing is worse than the punch to my gut he inflicted moments ago. My face contorts in pain. His eyes widen.

"Hey, I didn't mean to—"

The ringing of my mobile cuts him off. I race towards the sound of Thyra's ringtone. Snatching my mobile up and putting it on speaker, I shout for her to speak.

"Get your asses back here! I found Blaise."

CHAPTER 8

olin

MY HEART POUNDS HARDER than my feet as we race from the gym back to Thyra's office. At last, she found that fucker, and we can get Signy back. I pray to the gods she's all right. But no matter what, we will ensure she has the medical and mental care she needs. Then we'll claim her. Signy is ours.

Viggo's howl echoes around us. We don't pause, even after Jagger's responding call reaches us from nearby.

We rush into the building and down the hallway. Thyra's door stands open, awaiting our return. We hurry inside. She grins from ear to ear and points to her monitors. We crowd around her. This time, she doesn't protest our nearness.

"I picked up on messages from the Dark Web. Code-names—not so subtle—made me dig further. Apparently, a new *shipment* arrived, and Blaise went to retrieve it since it's so large. He's—"

"Where is she?"

"What did you find out?"

"Is she okay?"

Jagger, Dolph, and Rust storm into the office. Naked as the day they were born, they rush to the desk and peer over Thyra's shoulder. She rolls her eyes but refrains from a snarky comment. Instead, she continues.

"He's in Maine. In a remote area south of the Canadian border. Satellite images depict several trucks and a structure. At least forty males on the ground. Heavily armed."

She points to two monitors with satellites trained on the property. The place crawls with males carrying semi-automatic weapons and combat gear. The *shipment* must be valuable for them to be so prepared to defend it.

But is Signy amongst those captured? Or is she someplace else?

I swear, once we have her, she's getting a tracker implanted. We'll never lose her again. This shit is killing me.

"Do you have visuals on the she-wolves?"

Garrett's question cuts into my thoughts. I tune back in.

Thyra shakes her head.

"I checked the past feed. But it only shows the trucks arriving. Males enter and leave from the rear. No signs of the females. The structure is where the males must sleep. The shipment arrived a couple of days ago. Helicopters arrived with Blaise and his crew, I assume."

Beeps from another monitor draw everyone's attention. Thyra swivels in her chair to face it. She gasps.

"What?!" I shout.

"An auction."

A collective growl reverberates around the office. Each male mutters curses.

"When?" Jagger barks.

Thyra scans the messages.

"In two days… They're sending invitations to interested parties along the East coast… Bidding will occur on site with pick up immediately after deposits of winning bids… Thirty she-wolves… Ten humans, not turned yet. My gods. You must save them."

She stares over her shoulder at her older brother. Imploring eyes meet his, flashing in anger. They exchange a silent communication through Garrett's Alpha bond, and she nods before turning back to the monitors. Her fingers fly across the keyboard. The printer churns out pages. She snatches them up and hands them to him.

"These are the coordinates along with a list of those who RSVP'd. Assholes. Their names are in code. But you can get the details from Blaise when you snatch him.

You'll need to keep him alive to find Signy's location in case she's not with this group. And to glean information from him about any other activities. What a dirty dog!"

Bile rises in my throat at the thought of Signy on a stage up for auction as a breeding she-wolf. Our virgin mate for sale. Hell. No.

"Jagger, you and I need to communicate with the other Alphas. Aspen is the closest and can send enforcers. We'll need some from Miami too," Garrett says.

"Already on it to Tag, my beta," Jagger responds with his mobile to his ear.

"Let's go to my office," Garrett says, then turns to us. "Dolph, speak to Arne to cover while we're gone, then come to my office. Colin, gather the enforcers in the meeting hall and get the weapons loaded onto the heli-copters."

"Viggo and Rust with me. Dylan with Colin," Jagger commands.

We file out.

"Tell me what you need. I've got your back," Dylan says as we jump into an SUV.

"Thanks, brother," I respond as I send a group text to the enforcers to gather. Message sent, I start the ignition and drive towards the artillery warehouse. "We'll get the weapons ready. If we didn't need Blaise for information, I'll stick a rocket up his ass and set it off."

Dylan claps his sizable hands.

"I'm all for it. He'll learn not to fuck with ours. And the

gods help him if he hurt Signy. She's a little sister to me. I will tolerate no one messing with her. No. One."

He adds the last words as he cocks an eyebrow at me.

I nod since I can't argue with him. We did mess up.

By the time we're finished loading the helicopters, Garrett calls to join them in the meeting hall for the briefing. Energy sparks through me. Time for action at last.

DOLPH

"I WISH we were gathering under more pleasant circumstances, my friends. But we'll get this behind us and celebrate the return of Signy to her loved ones and the destruction of Blaise's ring. These breeders are getting out of hand all over. Too many suspicious disappearances in my territory, too. We have to stop them. Now."

The Aspen Wolves Pack Alpha Leif Karlsson clasps Garrett and Jagger on their backs as he enters Garrett's living room. The Aspen wolves arrived en masse within hours of the call to them, as did enforcers from Miami.

We have well over one hundred enforcers to combat Blaise. And we'll need them. Thyra's latest projections show the bidders arriving, increasing the numbers present in Maine. Plus, we'll need a fresh unit ready to rescue Signy if she's not amongst the stolen females.

The unit headed for Maine leaves in an hour after Garrett briefs Leif and the other newcomers. As Garrett's beta, I will travel with him. Colin will wait here to lead the second unit. He grumbled about not being on the ground in Maine in case Signy is there. But Garrett assured him we'll bring Blaise and Bernard back alive to torture the truth from them.

Meanwhile, Thyra will continue to monitor the Dark Web for clues to Signy's whereabouts. They highly prize the daughter and sister of Alphas. Plus, Blaise knows she's the fated mate of another Alpha. Her association to two powerful wolf packs makes her the perfect breeder of future Alphas. Chatter will be rampant for her. Fuckers.

"I agree with you, my friend," Garrett says as Jagger agrees. They proceed to fill Leif in on the plan.

Soon, we're aboard the helicopters bound for Maine. Adrenaline rushes through me. Mind alert. Body pumped. We're coming for you, Blaise.

An hour and a half later, we land in the remote forest of the Allagash Wilderness Waterway. Dense growth of trees and foliage provide the perfect location for a clandestine auction—and an ambush. We arrive under the cover of night. The sky filled with millions of stars, but no moon to cast light on our approach. Stealth mode.

We move as well-trained units broken out by pack since they're used to each other's tactics. From three sides, we converge on the property nestled in a clearing surrounded by evergreens. Snow covers the ground. A primitive campsite with a building in the center and a couple of outhouses. The trucks form a semicircle around the structures. SUVs and helicopters stand to the side. Men with weapons strapped to their bodies and in their hands patrol the area.

Shoulder to shoulder, Garrett and I lead our enforcers —some in wolf form—to the trucks while the other two packs set their sights on the structures and the vehicles. No one will get away from us. Especially Blaise and Bernard, as they did months ago during our first encounter, where we only came away with their now dead techie.

My wolf paces, eager to come forth, ready to fight for our fated mate. But I keep him under control. I want to feel the pain I'll inflict on theses fuckers with my hands. I tighten my grip on the knives at my waist. We'll use them, guns with silencers, and fangs to minimize noise and the announcement of our presence.

Garrett raises a fist—the signal to stop. We await his command to move forward once the caw of a crow from Jagger and the hoot of an owl from Leif sound. Moments later, the *birds* call out. We rush towards the trucks.

Unsuspecting enemies fall one after the other. We leave a trail of the dead in our wake. Blood splatters on the pristine snow. I open the back of the nearest truck and hop inside, followed by Garrett. The stench of body fluids and fear assaults my nostrils. Cages stacked atop one another line the interior. Frightened eyes peer at me from behind the wire sides. Sobbing starts. I shake my head and bring a finger to my lips.

"Hush. We're here to rescue you," Garrett says. When they quiet down, he continues. "Is Signy Larson here?"

We rush from cage to cage, asking for Signy. No one knows her.

Dammit!

We tell them to remain quiet while we finish the males outside. Their soft cries of relief touch my heart. But not having Signy amongst them shatters it. We leave enforcers to guard the females before we escort them to our helicopters.

I follow Garrett as he jumps from the truck and runs to the other one. The sounds of fighting fill the night— howls, gunshots, screams. I ignore them solely focused on reaching the other truck as I pray to the gods Signy is in it.

One of our enforcers hops down from the truck. Before we can ask, he shakes his head. No Signy.

Fuck!

Where the hell can she be?

Garrett and I exchange glances, then race for the building. We have to get Blaise and Bernard.

"Where the fuck is my sister?!"

Jagger's angry roar punches through the sounds of fighting.

Garrett and I increase our speed.

Jagger and Viggo stand over Blaise and Bernard. The scent of burning flesh mingles with the blood. Silver handcuffs hold their wrists and silver shackles bind their ankles as they sit on the ground at the brothers' feet.

Viggo kicks Blaise's arm. The steel-toe boot cracks the bone. The male howls in pain.

"Answer my brother, or I'll rip your arm off and beat you with the bloody stump," Viggo growls.

"Fuck. You."

Bernard screams in agony as Jagger's extended claws rake across his face. The flesh parts like hot butter. Blood pours from the gashes. Unfortunately, his enhanced healing knits the skin closed. No matter, Jagger slashes him again, and new cuts form, while Bernard drops to his side muttering curses in French.

"This is only the beginning. I will cause unimaginable pain, let you heal, and hurt you again, repeatedly. You'll beg for a silver bullet between the eyes," Jagger growls.

"Jagger."

He pauses, hand raised, blood dripping from his claws as Garrett calls his name.

The walkie-talkie crackles at Garrett's hip.

"The bidders are secure," Leif announces.

"Excellent. Let's take this party back to The Fortress. We have some torture to perform," Garrett says.

A chilling grin spreads across Jagger's face.

"And so it begins," he says, and yanks Blaise to his feet.

Garrett

"No, Signy isn't here. We're on our way to The Fortress with Blaise, Bernard, and the bidders. The others are dead. The females will go to the infirmary. A cleanup crew stayed behind. Hang tight. We'll keep you posted."

I end the call with Colin and lean back in my seat on the helicopter.

"I'm sure Colin is ripping his hair out by now," Dolph says. "I can't say that I blame him."

"Yeah," I say, then shift my gaze to Blaise in the seat opposite mine. He glares back it me, silent since we took off.

Bernard sits across the aisle opposite Jagger and Viggo. We want the fuckers close to avoid any surprises. My fingers flex, eager to get my hands on them. One hand forms a fist and shoots out to punch Blaise's nose. Bones crunch on impact. Blood spurts. Dopamine floods my system at his pained yowl.

"You like to beat on females and force them against their will? You'll soon know what it's like to face a male, one stronger than you," I growl.

I turn at a scream from across the aisle. Jagger smirks as he flexes his fingers. Bernard spits out a few teeth from his bloody mouth.

"That's the truth," Jagger says.

An hour later we land within the walls of The Fortress.

Enforcers line the path to the front doors. The doctor and nurse standby for the females to land. I nod at them as we pass.

Dolph and I lead our captives, including the bidders and the others, to the dungeons. We reach the secured silver doors that lead below. I enter the code and slip a protective glove over my hand to open the doors. They shut behind us, and I tuck the glove in the side pocket of my cargo pants. We make our way down the stairs and enter a code into a second set of doors. They open to a monitoring room where two enforcers watch the camera feeds through the dungeons.

"Hello, Alpha. We have the cells ready for our *guests*," they say as they rise from their seats at the long desk.

"Perfect," I respond and continue to the final set of doors buzzed open by one enforcer. Silence descends as the doors shut. The temperature drops to barely warm.

As we pass rows of cells on each side of the corridor, we push a *guest* inside and the door slides shut. Unlike the original unlit stone walls and floors with metal bars facing the corridor, these cells are all steel with silver bars.

Lights along the corridor ceiling illuminate the cells. Whomever is inside has no choice but to sleep under the glare of the lights. Too damn bad.

We walk to the end of the corridor beyond the last two cells. I open the door for the corridor to the interrogation rooms. My heart races with adrenaline as I envision all we'll do to Blaise and Bernard. As Jagger said, *and so it begins.*

Unable to withstand our… methods, the fuckers cave. I call Thyra with the coordinates, and she confirms satellite footage of the property in Pownal, Vermont set in the Green Mountain National Forest shows a farmhouse, barn, and males. Colin roars. His boots pound the floor as he runs from her office. Without a doubt, he's bound for Signy.

We dump Blaise and Bernard into separate cells. I command the enforcers to maintain a visual on them and the bidders at all times, rotate shifts as necessary until I return to handle them. We leave the dungeons and race for the helicopters.

We're on our way to you, Princess.

CHAPTER 9

olin

"Listen, Garrett, I respect you as my pack Alpha and my Commanding Officer. However, you cannot stop me from rescuing our fated mate now. We don't have time to waste—"

"Dylan, get my sister the fuck out of that shit hole. Right. Now. I don't give a fuck what Garrett says!"

This is the one time I have to agree with Jagger and side against my best friend. I'm not waiting. We're five minutes from the location. We hit the ground running. Period.

"I agree, Garrett. You know what it's like for these females," Dolph says, also over the speakerphone.

A beat later, Garrett gives in.

"Fine. We're twenty minutes out. Take care of our mate, Colin. Or you'll have hell to pay," he growls.

I end the call.

"Let's get our girl!" Dylan says.

We land a safe distance away from the property. Enforcers from all three packs follow my lead as we stealthily close in on the farmhouse and the barn.

Fewer males guard the area since they had the auction to cover. Obviously, the more expensive lot takes precedence over the females they already have, including Signy. Our gain. Their loss. We end them one by one.

Dylan with the Miami pack secured the barn. I sprint to it since the odor of females emanates from the dilapidated building. Of course, Blaise would treat them like livestock. And the stench that hits my nose when I reach the open doors attests to his less than caring attitude towards the females.

I glance around frantically for a glimpse of Signy's ebony black waist-length hair or her ice blue eyes. Dylan jogs towards me from the rear. He shakes his head.

"She's not in here, and none of them recognize her name," he says.

"The farmhouse," we say in unison and race across the field where the Aspen pack secured the building.

"Signy!" I bellow as I run through the front door. "Signy! Are you in here?"

"Colin? Oh, Colin! Thank the gods!"

My knees buckle at the sound of her voice at the top of the staircase. I grip the banister and stare up at her. My heart lurches in my throat at the sight of my fated mate in a black long-sleeve t-shirt and bare legs.

An Aspen male wolf shifter stands shirtless beside her, his arm around her waist. She leans into him. He takes several steps back as a possessive growl bursts forth from the depths of my chest.

My eyes flash gold with my wolf near the surface. I bound up the stairs four at a time.

"Signy!" I rasp as I grab her in my arms and pull her flush to my body. I bury my face in her hair and inhale a lungful of her unique scent. The forest after a spring rain, woody and earthy, with a hint of wild honey straight from the comb.

"Are you all right? Did… Did they hurt you?" I choke out. "Oh, gods, you're safe now, my mate. Safe."

Tears dampen my shirt as she cries against my chest. Her body trembles with her sobs. I squeeze her tighter, never wanting to let her go. Ever.

She nods.

My stomach drops.

I'll kill that motherfucker! Red clouds my vision.

"I—I'm okay, Colin. They never… touched me," she responds between sobs. "Thank the gods you're here."

Then she pulls back. Frantic eyes stare up at me.

"But Blaise said he'll be back! We have to go! Now! Hurry!"

She nearly stumbles down the stairs in her haste to get away.

I grip her waist tighter and draw her back to my side. My fingertips slide hair from her wide eyes.

"No, he won't be back. Garrett, Dolph, and the others captured him. He's locked away in the dungeons at The Fortress. That's how we learned your location."

Her mouth drops open as her eyes scan my face for any sign of an untruth. Satisfied, she sags against me and wraps her arms around my waist, burying her face against my chest again. Her shoulders shudder as she cries some more.

I scoop her into my arms and carry her down the stairs and out into the night. Dylan steps aside to let us pass.

"Signy!"

Five males call her name.

She raises her head from my shoulder and sobs harder at the sight of Garrett, Dolph, Jagger, Viggo, and Rust. Her hand covers her mouth.

I hold her tighter, not willing to let her go.

Mine!

A growl rumbles in my chest.

Signy tilts her heart-shaped face up to me.

"It's okay. You saved me, Colin. Thank you," she whispers. Her eyes glisten with more tears. "Let the others see I'm all right. Okay?"

I hesitate and glance at them as they approach. My

gaze returns to Signy. She nods in encouragement. I take a deep breath and nod back. But I don't set her down.

"Are you all right?"

"Did they hurt you?"

"Thank the gods!"

"We were out of our minds."

"Tell me you're okay."

They crowd around us. Fingers touch her face and arms., stroke her hair. Hands clutch her face. As they murmur words of love and gratitude. Rust drapes a blanket over her. Jagger steps away to call their parents and returns with them on speakerphone. They too tell her how much they love her and can't wait to see her. All the while, I never let her go.

Garrett and Dolph know better than to try to extract her from my hold. They flank me and press kisses to her face.

Viggo, Rust, and Dylan stand in front of me. Smiles split their faces. Jagger ends the call with their parents and nods.

"You're good, little sis? For real?" He asks as his ice blue eyes pin hers. "Tell me the truth. You don't have to be afraid."

Once again, she shakes her head. He inhales sharply. Then she corrects herself.

"I'm fine, Jagger. They slapped me around a few times" —growls erupt—"But it helped to jar my memory. I remember everything."

Everyone gasps, just now realizing she recognized her family. So caught up in the reunion, we didn't notice she called them by name.

Thank the gods for one bit of goodness that came from her ordeal.

"Also, because a special she-wolf helped me."

Signy squirms to get down. I don't want to let her go, but she's adamant. I relent but keep her close to my side. She glances around, then waves.

Our gazes follow her line of vision. An older she-wolf emerges from the farmhouse. She stares down as she steps over the worn planks carefully. The scent of cinnamon and apples carries on the wind. My heart clenches, recognizing the scent before my brain registers it. She raises her gaze. Tawny eyes meet tawny eyes. Her lower lip wobbles. Her step falters.

In a flash, I catch her as she crumples.

A shaky hand reaches up and cups my cheek.

"Colin, my child. I'm so very sorry."

Now, my knees give out. Strong hands grip my arms and the she-wolf before we land on the snowy ground. Tears stream down her gaunt cheeks. She raises her hand and wipes the wetness from mine. Shocked, I flick my gaze to her fingertips.

I'm… crying?

"Mama? Is that really you?"

She sobs and nods her head.

"Yes, Colin, my child. It's your mama. And I never

want to be away from you and your father again. That is, if you will have me in your lives after… after all this time."

My chest tightens at the realization she must have been a breeding she-wolf. Twenty years. Two decades trapped with these fuckers. Going through the gods only know what while my father and I hated her for abandoning us.

I drop my head in shame.

The better question is, will she have us in her life? Thank the gods my father never re-mated. Perhaps we can begin again as a family. The nine-year-old boy in me hopes his dream will come true.

Too overwhelmed to speak, I bend down and cradle my mother in my arms. I nod at Dolph and Garrett. He already holds Signy clutched to his chest. In silence, we march to the helicopters for the ride home to Moen Island.

I hope my father will be as understanding of my mother's unexpected capture and return.

CHAPTER 10

igny

"I'M JUST SO glad they're not here. But I worry when they come back… What they'll do to me. It's just so awful. If you weren't here with me, I don't know what I'd do."

My sentence ends in a whisper.

Estrid nods and pats my arm as we sit on the bed. A tray of food rests between us. She's determined to keep my strength up, telling me it's for the best. She knows since she survived twenty years in the brutal world of breeding rings.

Over the past two days, we shared more about ourselves. The relief on her face when I told her Colin is a handsome and brave male made my heart clench. I don't have news for her about her mate Brandt. But she's thankful to learn more about her now grown pup. I fill her in with as much as I know.

She tells stories from his birth to his childhood. His first shift into a tawny ball of fluff. Trying to dodge raindrops. Winning the spelling bee and strutting around with the ribbon pinned to his shirt for weeks. Happiness glows in her amber eyes. For a moment, she looks younger and at ease.

I can't help but to smile along with her.

However, with another night ending, I worry Blaise and Bernard will return, and I'll awake to that monster in the bed with me. A shudder racks through my body at the obscene thought.

"There's nothing you can do. Remember to drift away to your happy place. Don't let them get past the armor of your loved ones. And I'll be here for you—"

A series of loud cracks pop off outside the window. Males shout as howls fill the air. Glass shatters.

Estrid and I dive off the bed away from the broken window. We stare at one another with frightened eyes. She shakes her head and places a finger to her lips.

Who's out there?

I recall her tales of breeder rings invading others to kidnap the females for themselves. My stomach drops at the thought they'll drag us away to another hellish place. This time to one run by those unknown by Garrett,

Dolph, and Colin. They'll never rescue us. I'll never see my family again.

A sob rises from my chest as tears well in my eyes. Gods! I can't take anymore.

Shouts from below reach us. Gunfire erupts inside the farmhouse. Snarls rend the air while claws scrabble on the hardwood floors.

We duck under the bed. Eyes focus on the closed door. Estrid clutches my hand and motions for me to quiet. I nod, even though I want to run away screaming.

This is madness!

A loud thud outside the door makes us jolt.

I hold my breath as the door hinges squeak in protest. A pair of black combat boots appear and stride into the bedroom. Estrid's hand trembles in mine. Her face pales. I bite my tongue to prevent a scream from escaping as the boots stop at the foot of the bed. The male inhales.

"Signy? Is that you?"

An unfamiliar wolf shifter calls my name.

My head snaps around to stare at Estrid. Wordlessly, we debate whether I should answer. It could be a trick. A test to see if we'll try to escape. I don't trust that monster or his flunkies.

"Signy, I know you're under the bed. Come out. We don't have much time," the male says with urgency in his tone. "My name is Peter. I'm with the Aspen Wolf Pack, sent by my Alpha, your brothers, and your mates."

My heart skips a beat. Thank the gods!

I grin at Estrid. She nods and squeezes my hand. We crawl from beneath the bed. A firm hand hoists me to my feet. I reach back for Estrid. The male helps her.

"Are you okay to walk?" He asks as his gaze pings between us. He takes in the towel wrapped around me, then grips the back of his long-sleeve t-shirt and pulls it off.

I take it with a grateful smile.

He turns his back as I swap the towel for his shirt. It hangs to the middle of my bare thighs.

"Ready?" He asks without glancing back.

"Yes," Estrid and I respond in unison.

I stumble on the way out of the bedroom. He grips me by the waist and helps me while Estrid follows behind us. We reach the upper landing.

"Signy! Signy! Are you in here?"

My heart leaps in my chest. It's true. We're being rescued!

"Colin? Oh, Colin! Thank the gods!"

His eyes flick from me to the male who still steadies me. A spine-tingling growl fills the air before Colin leaps up the stairs. The male backs away from his ferociousness. I'm so thankful to see him. Tears blur my vision.

"Signy! Are you all right? Did… Did they hurt you? Oh, gods, you're safe now, my mate. Safe."

He holds me tight to his chest while my tears fall freely.

"I—I'm okay, Colin. They never… touched me. Thank the gods you're here."

Then I remember Blaise's threat before we left. I jerk away.

"But Blaise said he'll be back! We have to go! Now! Hurry!" I exclaim as I rush for the stairs. I stumble. But Colin catches me.

Relief washes over me when he says they're in The Fortress dungeons, far away from here. As he carries me out of the farmhouse, I hear my name called. Happiness fills me at the sight of my brothers, Garrett, and Dolph. Colin doesn't let me down—not that I blame him. So, they gather around. Jagger even gets our parents on his mobile. More tears pour from my eyes. I can't wait to see them.

I assure everyone I'm okay, then remember Estrid. If not for her, I would be in worse condition. She comes forward when I wave her over. I'll forever remember the moment Colin recognizes his mother, and she cups his face. It's such a poignant scene. I hope it helps to ease the horribleness she endured for so many years.

"I need to hold you, Princess."

Garrett's gruff voice murmurs in my ear before he scoops me into his arms. He presses his forehead to mine and inhales deeply. Dolph strokes my hair and presses his face against my neck. Cocooned by them, the pain and suffering of the last few days pales compared to the waves of emotions rolling off them. I close my eyes and sigh.

"Please take me away from here," I whisper.

"Absolutely," Garrett murmurs.

We move in silence to a helicopter. Once on board, Garrett bundles me in more covers and straps me into a seat next to him. Dolph sits across from us with Jagger. Colin and Estrid sit in the seats on the other side of the aisle with Rust. Viggo and Dylan sit behind us.

I watch the farmhouse and the barn disappear as we fly away. I want to close that chapter of my life forever. My eyes close on a sigh as I snuggle deeper into the buttery leather chair draped in covers. The last thing I feel before sleep takes me is Garrett's lips pressed to my temple.

"Rest easy, our mate."

My heart thumps in my chest.

Am I ready for that so soon after this ordeal?

I awake in Dolph's arms as he carries me from the helicopter. Sleepily, I glance around us. We're on an airstrip surrounded by a forest. Several hangars line one side. A caravan of SUVs waits on the other. The salty scent of the ocean fills my nostrils as the sound of waves in the distance reaches my ears. The stars are less plentiful in the inky sky.

"Welcome home to Moen Island, Baby Girl," Dolph murmurs with a smile as he carries me to an SUV.

Home? Is home on Moen Island or on Moon Island? With my Miami pack or their New York pack?

Even though I remember how my body responded to theirs, the attraction we shared—well, aside from Colin, who wasn't the most pleasant to me—I now have my memories back. I remember my parents, my brothers, my sisters-in-law, my nieces and nephews, my friends, my pack. Those who died in the jet crash. Why I came to New York in the first place to curate items from Fashion Week for my luxury online boutique Signy's Secret Cache.

Sure, I want a mate of my own to experience the love my brothers share with their fated mates. But I never accounted for three! My traitorous body reacts to the memories of Garrett and Dolph giving me carnal pleasure and the thrill of Colin's closeness when he taunted me. My nipples pucker as my pussy flutters.

But I only know them as the woman with no memories and no idea she's a wolf shifter. Not as Signy the Miami Pack Princess, beloved by all with hopes and dreams.

I need time. Time to recover from too many traumatic events in such a short period—the crash, amnesia, kidnapping, abuse. I need to see my parents and my family to hug them close as I thank the gods to be back with them and away from those monsters. Time to rethink my life and what I want to do with it. I have another chance, and I want to do what's best for me.

Dolph straps me to a seat next to Estrid, with Colin beside her. She smiles at me. I think of how she resented her rushed mating once she got to know her mate better. How she lost so much of her life because of one night.

I need time.

Garrett waits in the driver's seat for Dolph to hop in.

"Ready?" He asks with his eyes on me in the rearview mirror.

Am I ready? And for what?

Again, it's too much too soon.

My gaze slides away from his to stare out the window. I watch my brothers hop into another SUV. We drive off separately. Is this symbolic of what's coming? They go their way, and I go mine?

Gods, what do I do? Is something wrong with me to wonder about these things when Garrett, Dolph, and Colin risked their lives to save me?

I just don't know. My mind whirs as I watch the scenery go by.

~

Garrett

Signy is unusually quiet.

It's been a day since we rescued her. She chose to stay with her brothers in the guest house. Rust added his doctor's take on it and recommended he exams her fully and she spends time wherever she's most comfortable. Dolph, Colin, and I know she's been through a lot, so we left her with them.

Now, she sits in their living room on the sofa, tucked in blankets between Jagger and Viggo. The three of us sit on chairs opposite the siblings. An uncomfortable silence lies heavy in the air.

Jagger glances at Signy. An almost imperceptible nod from her, and he clears his throat.

"We thank you for helping to rescue Signy," he starts.

My stomach knots at his flat tone. I shift my gaze to her. But she keeps her head bowed, eyes on her hands in her lap. Dolph sits forward, resting his elbows on his knees. Colin cocks his head.

"We leave for Miami—"

"*We*, who?"

"What the hell?"

I sit silent as Dolph and Colin interrupt him.

"Signy—"

"You've gotta be kidding me!"

"We just got her back!"

The knot tightens to the point of pain. My eyes never leave Signy's face. She bites her lower lip as her fingers twist the cover.

"Signy needs to go home to Miami, have time to reconnect with our family and pack, to think about what she wants to do. It's decided," Jagger says with the finality of Alpha authority.

I ignore everyone in the room.

"Signy."

She jolts at me addressing her. But her eyes remain downcast.

"Signy," I repeat, using my Alpha command to force her eyes on me.

Immediately, her gaze lifts to meet mine. She presses her lips together.

"What do you want to do?"

She parts her lips, then closes them. Her throat works on a swallow. She tries again.

"I—I'm forever grateful you saved me. But so much has happened. My mind is reeling. I need time," she says, then rushes on after Colin groans. "Just a couple of weeks. Please."

I study her face.

She's so beautiful it hurts to look at her, knowing she wants to leave us. Although we're not bonded, my heart aches at the loss of her already. But I can't go back on my word.

"When the three of us realized you are our fated mate, you were still in the medically induced coma. I vowed as my Alpha duty to keep an eye on you, make certain you have the best care, and once you were awake, find out your identity. If you have a mate or want to return to your pack, I vowed to ensure you arrive to them safely. But if you sense the mate bond with us and want to stay with our pack, I will support your decision. And it's always been your choice. Even now."

Dolph sighs and sits back in his chair.

"I stand by my vow. You want to go home, Signy? I will

not stop you nor allow Dolph or Colin to interfere with your decision. Should you return, we will be here for you."

I rise from my chair—steady despite the pain crushing my chest—and gesture for Dolph and Colin to precede me from the living room and out of the guest house. They cast longing looks at Signy but follow my command.

Thirty minutes later, the three of us in wolf form stand on a bluff above the beach. The chilly wind ruffles our fur. The salty air fills our noses. Our flashing eyes stare up as we watch Jagger's private jet head south with our fated mate on board. We watch until it's no longer visible, lost in the inky sky.

As one, our heads tilt back. Mournful howls lift to the heavens as we plead with the gods.

You brought her to us on one jet.

She leaves us on another.

Will she return to us once again?

Or must we live in agony at the loss of Signy, our fated mate?

CHAPTER 11

olin

"WE'LL HAVE the bidders ready for transport... I will attend the Ruling Council meeting to decide their punishment which I believe should be death or at the very least castration with a dull silver blade... Definitely a lesson and a message to others who think they can abduct females, breed them, and sell their pups... Bastards... Blaise and Bernard will remain here at The Fortress until I deem otherwise. I want to glean all I can from them. They're the largest ring and a source for the other ones..."

I half listen as Garrett holds a video conference call with the Alphas from the Los Angeles, Sedona, and the

Las Vegas packs. Leif sits with us at the conference table in Garrett's office. Jagger's expressionless face stares at us from the flat-screen television on the wall.

I wonder where his sister is right now. Is she on the beach in a tiny bikini being ogled, or does she sit at home missing us?

Since Signy left, we returned here to sort out this mess. I wholeheartedly released my frustration and anger on each of those fuckers, including the bidders. Over the course of two days, they learned more than one *lesson* at my hands already.

"Yes, sixty-five females and twenty pups are getting the care they need, medical and mental. As expected, they are malnourished, dehydrated, abused in ghastly ways… Some are pregnant… I agree the turned females and those still human need special attention and packs to join… Perhaps place them in those closest to their homes… No, they can never contact their families again… The she-wolves will return to their packs once they're well enough to travel…"

My hands form fists as I recall the condition of the females. Frightened, bruised, maimed, filthy. Inconceivable. And my mother was amongst them. For twenty years. A growl rumbles in my chest.

The others glance at me. I close my eyes and take a deep breath.

My mother is safe now. On Moen Island recovering in the hospital. I hated to leave her so soon. But I had to come here and beat the shit out of the fuckers who had her. It's the least I could do to make up for her years of suffering.

Fortunately, my father accepted her back as his mate. On the helicopter ride to Moen Island, I called him and told him to meet me at the hospital. I didn't tell him why, for fear his bitterness would keep him from going. Instead, I told him we needed all enforcers—including the retired ones—on duty.

I waited for him beside my mother's bed, where she lay freshly bathed in a clean gown. As his massive frame filled the doorway, she gasped.

His nostrils flared. His chest expanded on a deep inhalation, detecting her scent. He narrowed his eyes as he scanned her face. They widened in surprise as her scent and image merged into that of his long-lost mate. Shocked, his knees buckled, and his hands gripped the doorframe. He bowed his head as his shoulders shook. The realization she was a female rescued from the breeder's ring hit him hard.

When she called his name softly, he raised a tear-stained face. Their eyes locked. Silent communication passed between them through their mate bond, unbroken after all these years. He took a ragged breath and stumbled to her bedside. His enormous body engulfed her tiny form as he pulled her into his arms. Careful of the IVs, he sat on the bed and positioned her on his lap, her head tucked under his chin as he closed his eyes. All the years of anger and bitterness melted away. Their love was palpable.

I had to step from the room to avoid intruding upon the intimacy of their reunion.

I left a note with a nurse to let them know I was going to The Fortress and would see them in a few days. The doctor said she wouldn't be ready to leave the hospital for a while, anyway. And with my father loving on her so hard, my reluctance to leave her lessened. He would care for his mate.

"It's no rumor. Signy Larson is the fated mate for Dolph, Colin, and for me... Yes, the three of us detected her unique scent when we found her at the crash site... No, we haven't claimed her. Yet... She's in Miami recovering from the ordeals she experienced... We will give her the time she needs. Enough with our love lives. You sound like a bunch of gossipy hens. That's all I have to report. If no other pertinent questions, this call is finished... Great. I'll see you at the Ruling Council meeting."

The screen darkens.

Garrett sits back and scrubs a hand over his face with a sigh.

"'Gossipy hens?' You pegged them right. I wish Signy and you well," Leif says and stands. "Now, we're off. This mission was an even better success since we recovered two of our she-wolves. They're eager to return to Aspen, and their families are ecstatic. Our pack doctor will care for them on our journey home. See you at the meeting, my friend."

He claps each of us on the back and strides from the office.

"I still can't believe she left us and hasn't made contact in days," Dolph says, as he rubs his chest with the heel of his hand.

The gesture is familiar to me as the ache in my heart grows with each passing day. The constant thrum serves as a reminder our fated mate isn't near. Thousands of miles separate us. She might as well be on another planet at the far end of the universe.

"Her choice. Period."

Garrett's response irks me.

Sure, Signy should have a say about what happens in her life. However, her decision impacts us too. We may not have completed our bonding by issuing our claiming bites on her. But the connection exists. Created by the gods as what is meant to be. The ache of separation runs deep.

Unconsciously, my fist presses against my heart.

The movement catches Garrett's eye. He flicks his gaze from me to Dolph, gaze focused on our hands. He brings his own to rub the ache he feels, too. Not one of us can deny it or ignore it. And it won't go away until Signy is back with us as our claimed mate.

I rise abruptly. The chair skitters behind me across the floor.

"My job here is done. I'm going back to Moen Island to spend time with my mother. At least I now know she didn't abandon me because she chose to leave."

The jab isn't lost on Garrett and Dolph.

Yeah, I'm pissed Signy made a selfish decision. It's messed up on so many levels. We saved her from the fiery crash, provided her with the best treatment, kept her fed and sheltered, and rescued her from ending up like my mother.

We deserve more than thanks and goodbye now that I regained my memory. I'm going home with my big brothers to be with my mommy and my daddy. See ya, fellas!

How could she do that?

Sure, I was a dick to her at times. But it was from fear of reliving the pain of abandonment by a loved one again. And it happened anyway. Great.

I will not mope around like Dolph or be gallant like Garrett. No. I'm pissed.

"You two can stay here. I'm out."

I pivot on my boot heel and stomp from the office.

On the way to the helipad, I call my father to check on my mother and to let him know I'm on my way to the hospital. He assures me she's doing better than the last time I saw her. Her body frail and small in the bed, hooked to machines and IV drips. Dark shadows under her eyes, in stark contrast to her pale skin. The only sign of the beautiful young mother I remember are her tawny eyes like mine.

I thank the gods she's home safe and recuperating quickly. With the constant flow of IV fluids and plenty of rest, her enhanced wolf healing recharges. To increase her recovery., the doctor wants her to shift. She needs to gain more strength for her body to handle the powerful trans-formation.

The captors didn't allow her to shift in all that time—twenty years stuck in her human form. Hopefully, her body will remember how to call forth her wolf and to accept the change of her body's makeup. Ordinarily, the shift doesn't hurt. But with all the years that passed, who knows if she will have a painless transformation. I pray she does. She doesn't need any more pain in her life.

The helicopter ride to the island lasts less than half an hour. I stride into her hospital room shortly after I end the call with my father. They smile as I enter.

"Mama, you look well!"

She smiles and her eyes shine golden as she pats the bed next to her.

"Thank you, Colin, my child. Come sit with your mother."

Like my nine-year-old self, I lope over to her bed and sit on the edge, mindful of the IVs and other attachments. She hugs me to her bosom and ruffles my hair like she used to do. My arms wind around her.

Tears prick at the backs of my eyes as I lose myself in her loving embrace. My Mama is back. She's safe. I'll never let her out of my sight. Unlike Signy.

"What's on your mind?"

I flinch, surprised she picked up the flare of anger. Not wanting negativity to interrupt our moment, I shake my head.

She pulls back and cups the sides of my face, aligning our gazes. Her eyes probe mine. I avert them. But she's insistent and ducks her head to follow me.

"Oh, Colin, we may have been apart for years. But I know you, my child. You could never hide your emotions from me."

I quirk my lips and lift a shoulder, a habit of mine when I didn't want to answer my mother's questions.

"How's Signy? Is your fated mate recovering okay? I haven't seen her, and no one mentions her to me."

My mother lets her hands fall to her lap as I stand.

I grip the back of my neck and stride to the window. A light snowfall blows in the wind. I lift my gaze to the gray sky.

Is Signy enjoying the sunny weather in Miami?

Obviously, she's seen enough snow.

"She went with her brothers, didn't she?"

Pain sears my heart. I close my eyes and rub my chest. My head hangs. Forehead presses to the windowpane.

"Oh, sweetheart. Come. Sit with me. I need you to hear what I have to tell you."

I return to her side. She sits up higher in the bed.

My father fluffs the pillows behind her back. She graces him with a beatific smile. His gray eyes glow silver. Again, they communicate in silence. He lowers back to his chair and holds her hand. She smiles at him and turns her attention to me.

"Signy and I spoke for hours. We shared things about ourselves, hopes and dreams. She acknowledges the three of you as her fated mates."

My heart skips a beat as hope blooms.

"But you must realize she's been through so much in such a short period. She explained how frightened she was after realizing she lost her memory. She felt alone in the world with no history, no family. Can you imagine what she experienced?"

I consider my mother's words. To lose all that I know that makes me who I am would be tough to handle. I'm a strong male who's faced and doled out death. But the idea of not knowing me is frightening.

"No, Mama, I can't," I admit.

She nods and pats my hand.

"I told her how my mating to your father was fast and followed by your birth just as quickly and how my focus on the two of you left me resentful," she says and pauses to study my reaction.

My eyebrows lift to my hairline as my head jerks back. I recall my parents arguing when they thought I was asleep in bed. But I never suspected she resented her role as mate and mother.

"Don't misunderstand. I loved your father and you dearly. I just felt I lost myself in caring for the two of you and not taking time for me. Had I stopped and focused on what I wanted, things may have happened differently. I will forever regret my actions that led to heartache for the three of us."

I squeeze her hand.

"Mama, don't blame yourself for what those monsters did to you. You had every right to spend time in the city. They were wrong for kidnapping you and causing us heartache. I was angry since I didn't know why you left us. But I never stopped loving you. And love you even more now."

Tears slip down her cheeks. My father dabs her face with a tissue.

"We're beyond the past. We have our future together," he says gruffly, as tears shine in his eyes.

I nod as my mother presses her cheek against his palm.

She lifts her gaze to me.

"Let Signy have the time she needs to reconnect with her family, with her memories, and to decide what she wants. Don't force her to have to lose herself for your gain. Your father and I may not be a fated pair. However, the pain of our separation lasted until he walked through that door. Signy is your fated mate. She feels as you do and will not stay away from the three of you for long. Trust in your bond."

I close my eyes and absorb my mother's wise words.

Okay, Signy, we'll give you the time you need.

For now.

CHAPTER 12

olph

SEVEN DAYS. Fourteen hours. Thirty seconds.

My golden wolf's wide paws pound through the underbrush of the forest on Moen Island. We leap over fallen tree trunks. Dart around boulders. Zip between bushes. We run for miles.

But we can't outrun the incessant ache from the loss of our mate.

Garrett and I listened to Colin tell us about his mother's recommendation. We heeded her advice. Hell, my mother told me the same thing. *Give Signy time.*

We haven't heard from her. At. All.

Garrett—Mr. I'm Not Going Back On My Vow—

invoked Alpha authority and told Colin and me we can't initiate communication with her. She has to make the first move. *Her choice. Period.*

Fuck. Me.

And my heart isn't the only organ aching.

My cock stays hard, more than it's flaccid. Wake up to a woodie. Jerk off in the shower. A thought of Signy's sweet pussy. Hard as steel. Go to bed with my fist pumping until I gush like a geyser all over my abs and chest. A fucking breeze blows, and my junk jumps to attention. Absolute agony.

Even now, my cock stiffens. Do you know how hard—pun intended—it is to run with a fifth leg? Very.

I slow to a trot, then throw myself down beneath a giant fir tree. Its low-hanging boughs provide shelter from the chilly gusts off the Atlantic Ocean. The pine needles offer a soft blanket to rest on. My tongue lolls from my panting mouth as my flanks heave from the exertion of my endless run.

How I wish Signy were beside me. I'd rise behind her, grip her fur-covered neck between my teeth, forelegs along her flanks, and impale her with my thick cock. Her howls spur me to thrust deeper, harder until my knot forms at the base of my cock and locks her to me while my seed fills her womb. We'd lay on our sides connected as one until my knot deflates and my cock slips from her wet warmth. She'd curl into a ball, and I'd curl around her, cocooned in bliss.

Fuck!

That vision did not help my current situation. Instead, my cock pulsates as more blood surges to harden it further. I growl in frustration and shift.

Immediately, my hand fists around the base of my shaft and squeezes. My head lolls back as I pump my fist up my length and palm the mushroom-shaped tip. The pre-cum acts as a natural lubricant to slicken the downward stroke. Groans pour from my slack mouth as I beat my junk.

My heavy balls draw up. The ladder of my abs contract. My pace quickens. Grip tightens. With an almighty roar of Signy's name, I cum harder than I ever have before. Thick, creamy ropes of jizz shoot from the slit at the tip. Bright lights explode behind my closed eyelids. My body convulses with each pulse of cum from my cock. I sprawl backwards as my chest heaves with my pants.

I pretend Signy licks the cum from my hand before she sucks each finger clean. Her little pink tongue flicks each digit as her hooded eyes—darkened to cobalt—lock with my flashing golden ones.

Once she finishes, I toss her onto her back. Arms and legs flail. I shoulder my way between her silky thighs and return the favor. My tongue laps at her sweet juices and swirls around her engorged clit. Her hips roll to chase her orgasm. I blow cool air on her heated, slick folds. She writhes and calls my name as she begs me to let her cum.

After my fill of her bounty, I suckle her clit and thrust three fingers into her tight pussy. Her inner walls grip them like a vise. I groan as she moans deep in her throat. A nip to her clit sends her over the edge. My name a prayer from her lips as her back bows and her fingernails claw the earth. I lap at her gushing juices, collecting every drop on my tongue as I ease her down from the toe-curling orgasm. Mini ones follow in its wake. She collapses, sated.

The fantasy stiffens my cock. Again.

I growl in frustration and beat another release. Her name rips from my lips. Moments later, I shift and race through the forest, still attempting to outrun my need for my fated mate.

Garrett

SIGNY!

My jet black wolf skids to a stop at the roar of our mate's name. He cocks his head, recognizing Dolph's voice. My wolf snorts.

Yeah, we're not the only ones out here trying to work off sexual frustration.

Almost a week passed since Signy flew to Miami with her brothers, Dylan, and Rust. It's been radio silence. I expected she would at least call to tell us she made it to Moon Island safely. I won't say *home* since Moen Island is her home. New York, not Miami. Our pack, not Jagger's. My Luna and my mate. Shared with my best friends.

I know they're pissed at me for letting her go so easily. Not issuing an Alpha command to remain at our sides on Moen Island. Or arguing with Jagger to back the fuck off. Fighting for her, if necessary.

But I can't go back on my word. A male without honor is no male at all. From being raised by an Alpha to training at West Point to leading a Green Beret unit as their Captain and Commanding Officer and my pack as their Alpha, I learned my word is everything.

Did it pain me to watch Signy fly away from us?

Hell yes!

Dolph and Colin aren't the only ones who feel the ache in their hearts being separated from her. It's so intense, my claws threaten to tear into my chest cavity and rip my heart out to rid myself of the agony rippling through me. All. Day. Long.

A growl rumbles in my chest, vibrating with the pulses of pain.

Signy!

The growl deepens as Dolph roars again.

Enough!

My wolf darts in the opposite direction, racing to put distance between Dolph and us. The wind skims over the jet black fur. Sticks and leaves in patches of land no longer covered by snow snap and fly beneath huge paws. Our pulse races with each stride of the four long limbs as my wolf covers the ground quickly.

Moments later, a stream appears. Ice covers the edges while water glides over smooth, dark rocks in the center. My wolf trots to the ice and laps up the refreshing water. The chilly liquid flows down his throat. His tongue lolls out as his eyes scan the surrounding forest.

Moen Island doesn't have any predators other than our pack. Millennia ago, our ancestors dominated the land, leaving us as the apex predators. Which means an abundance of prey.

My wolf's head snaps to the left, attracted to the rustling of an animal on the other side of the stream. He tips his head back to scent the air. Wild turkeys. His superb vision detects the four-foot-tall birds as the flock moves towards the water's edge. They don't catch the scent of a predator since the wind blows from behind them towards my wolf.

Ordinarily, I'd let him hunt. But I'm not in the mood. A run to clear my head ranks higher than a meal. Besides, Thanksgiving passed. He doesn't appreciate my lame joke but doesn't protest when I urge him in the opposite direction. He casts a last glance at the big birds and lopes away.

He runs from one end of Moen Island to the other—a good nine miles. By the time we arrive at my mansion, my sore muscles scream for a hot shower. Happily, I oblige.

As I slip on a pair of gray joggers, my stomach rumbles.

I burned more calories than I ever have before. Wild turkey was off the menu. But I'm down for a Wagyu tomahawk steak. I enjoy the meal with cabernet sauvignon. It's satisfying to sit at my kitchen island eating a delicious dinner, albeit lonely, without my fated mate next to me.

I put the utensils and plate in the dishwasher and grab a glass and the bottle of wine. My bare feet pad across the heated hardwood floor to the living room. I drop a match on the kindling in the fireplace and lower myself onto the deep-seat leather sofa, feet up on the matching ottoman. I refill my wineglass and let my gaze settle on the fire.

Naturally, my mind drifts to a fantasy of Signy.

The glow from dozens of white candles of all shapes and sizes placed around the living room adds to the firelight. The air is fragrant with the scent of pine.

A heated smile crosses my face when I spot Signy lying on her back naked on top of the large faux-fur blanket before the stone fireplace. Her naked skin glows in the ambient red and orange light.

When she senses my presence, Signy bows her back and cups her full breasts, kneading them and plucking the beaded nipples. Her head thrown back as she moans deep in her throat.

Fuck. Me.

My cock expands in my joggers. The bulbous head pushes past the waistband. Like a divining rod, it seeks her wet, warm pussy. I shed the joggers with a quickness and prowl over to her. My eager dick bobs up and down in agreement as it slaps my eight-pack abs.

"Oh, Garret. I need you. Hurry," Signy purrs seductively, her eyes at half-mast.

As she licks her plump lower lip, she widens her bent knees. Fully on display for my viewing pleasure, her juicy pussy glistens and her puckered hole winks at me.

I sink down between Signy's welcoming thighs, placing my hands on her knees. Then I bend over her, so her pebbled nipples graze my hard chest.

"Tonight, I will take my time with you, my sweet Signy," I croon against her luscious lips.

She moans when I nip them and nudge my dick at her already slippery folds. Then we both groan when I sink myself inside her slowly.

I still to allow her body to accommodate my girth and deepen our kiss. Then shift my hips for long and even strokes, going further with each movement.

On a sigh, I trail open-mouthed kisses along Signy's neck down to her soft mounds. My lips latch onto her sensitive nipple and suckle strongly until she mewls and writhes beneath me, her hand pushing my head closer to her bosom.

My mouth glides across the hollow between her breasts to reach the other turgid nipple. Sucking hard on the bud until she squirms some more.

Signy cries out and lifts her hips to meet my thrusts as

I change to slow, shallow strokes. She wants it fast and deep.

But not tonight. No pounding into her. Tonight, I make sweet love to my fated mate.

I quiet Signy with a toe-curling kiss as I continue to rock into her hot, wet pussy in a gentle, steady rhythm. Her small hands clutch my thick biceps while her full breasts flatten between us, and her pelvis cradles mine. Our legs intertwine to bring us as close as possible intimately.

We continue to lose ourselves in the other as our climaxes build with the heat of our bodies, now warmer than the blazing fire beside us.

Signy gasps as her pussy clamps on my cock, sending an electric current up my length and through my body, zipping to my limbs. When her walls flutter and she begs for more, I increase my pace to thrust faster and deeper.

"Cum with me, baby! Cum hard with me now!" I thrum in her ear.

Signy bucks, then tightens all around me as her orgasm overtakes her.

The soft cries make my dick throb and pulse as I unleash a torrent of seed deep into her womb.

Together, we ride out our pleasure with kisses and words of love forever.

Caught up in the fantasy, my fist found my hard cock and stroked it through a spine-tingling release. Jizz covers my abs and thighs. I groan and throw my head back against the sofa.

"Gods, must you torture us?"

When they offer no response, I drag myself from the living room right back to the shower.

"Oh, Signy, Signy. You test my honor."

igny

"I'M glad you shared your business plan with me. Signy's Secret Cache is a fabulous idea! With your fashion sense and love of styling, this is your thing. You'll do so well!"

Sage—my sister-in-law married to Jagger and my Luna —grins as she exclaims over my project I haven't shared with anyone. Her emerald green eyes glitter like jewels set in her flawless toffee skin.

We sit on the back deck of their Spanish-style ten-thousand square foot bayfront mansion on Moon Island. The waters of Biscayne Bay glitter like diamonds around our pack's private island between South Beach on the barrier island and Edgewater on the coast. The tropical air carries a constant breeze of the Atlantic Ocean to lessen the humidity for a comfortable temperature. Its salty scent blends with the fragrance of the abundant jasmine and gardenia bushes. I close my eyes and inhale deeply and wonder how different it is here from Moen Island and the chilly, blustery north.

Images of Garrett, Dolph, and Colin appear behind my closed eyelids. Used to the cooler winter and because of our higher temperature as wolf shifters, they don't bother with too many layers. They're fine in parkas over long-sleeve t-shirts and cargo pants with combat boots. The added layer of their abundant muscles further protects them from the lower temperatures.

I can't say that I miss the weather. But not seeing them in person and spending time together these last six days wears a hole in my chest. A dull ache radiates from the center, stretching out from my heart. The tug of the mating bond?

Perhaps, if what I've heard my brothers and their mates mention when they're apart for too long. But they completed their bonding ceremonies—claiming bites, vows, consummation, and all. The four of us have not.

Who am I kidding?

I know I feel the pull on the burgeoning bond we share. And it's only gotten worse as more days pass with us apart. It must have been the intimate moments—or rather, the intense almost-fucking. My virgin pussy flutters at the memories of the virile males using their tongues, fingers, even teeth, to bring me to levels of erotic bliss I could never achieve on my own.

But am I ready to return to Moen Island and to the fated mates I left behind?

"Signy, I hear your brain whirring. What's on your mind?"

Sage's question draws me from my musings. Concern covers her gorgeous face as she peers into my eyes, into my very soul.

My eyes pop as I wonder if she read my mind.

She's a powerful immortal witch turned she-wolf with Jagger's claiming bite. She wields never-before-seen magick because of his DNA mixing with hers. As the High Witch of the Coven of the South and the head of the Witch Council, she governs all their kind. So, it's quite possible she heard my thoughts.

"Don't worry. I don't use my magick to read minds," she says, making me wonder even more. But I trust her implicitly.

I give her a sheepish smile before I respond.

"I don't know what to do about Garrett, Dolph, and Colin. I only know them as no-memory Signy and don't believe I can trust that judgement. What if the real me doesn't really like them?"

I pause as images of their handsome faces and mouth-watering tattooed bodies flash before my eyes. Yeah, what's not to like? Then I shake my head to clear the lustful thoughts. Be serious and get some answers!

"Do you foresee me having a good life with them?"

She purses her lips as her curly ebony hair sways from the firm shake of her head.

"I'm not a carnival fortuneteller either. I do not use my magick to answer relationship questions. You know me better than that, Signy," she admonishes.

With a sigh, I sag back on my chaise lounge.

"However, I will offer you advice."

I perk up.

"How can you know if you like them as you with all of your memories and knowledge of what you want in a mate if you're here and they're there?"

She arches a perfectly shaped eyebrow.

I consider her words. She's not wrong. I ran away before I had enough time with them as me.

"You sense the fated mate bond. Trust the gods' choices for you," she adds.

My gaze turns to glistening Biscayne Bay.

Is it time for me to return to the northern Atlantic Ocean?

Hours later, I sit on my bed, still pondering my next move when my mobile rings. A glance at the screen reveals a 917 mobile number from New York City. Could it be Garrett or Dolph, maybe Colin?

My hand hovers over the green accept button. What if it is one of them? What will they say? Will they be angry with me for leaving? Is it a sign I should fly back?

I close my eyes and press to accept the call.

"How are you doing, child?"

Estrid's voice surprises me. I release a stuttering breath.

"Oh, Estrid! Me? How are you?"

"Much better, especially with my mate Brandt by my side. The power of love heals all," she responds. Her choice of words makes my heart clench. "I called to check on you and to let you know *your* fated mates miss you."

And there it is. What I needed to know.

"I miss them, too," I whisper as my voice wobbles and tears spring to my eyes.

"Think of what you're going to do, child. Remember how precious time is and to cherish the ones you love every single day."

We end the call, and I crawl under my covers, determined to make my decision in the morning.

"Babe… Babe… Signy, wake up… I miss you so much."

Can I be dreaming? Or do I really hear Colin's voice? The deep rumble of his baritone rolls over me. It ignites a fire to lick across my skin, straight to my needy core. Oh, God, please let it be true…

Slowly, I open my eyes and roll over onto my back. Leaning on my elbow, I stare toward his voice. Even in the darkened room, I can distinguish Colin's sizable frame.

He stands at the foot of the bed. A swath of light from the moon crosses his face as the gauzy curtains flutter in the wind. His handsome face brightens as our eyes meet.

Full, kissable lips part as he licks the bottom one with the tip of his tongue.

I close my eyes and envision that tongue and mouth on my suddenly engorged clit. A moan slips past the lips on my face even as the lower ones swell with a desperate, aching need.

It's been way too long.

Seven excruciating days without the male I now realize I love. And want. Forever.

Thank the gods he's really here.

Colin's wicked chuckle rouses me from my pitiful musings. He glances down at my bare leg resting atop the sheets, then places one finger on the inside of my ankle. As he trails the tip along my instep, I moan aloud.

"You've been a naughty girl, *My Princess,*" he murmurs.

I gasp at the pressure he applies with his knuckle to the sole of my foot.

His tawny eyes flash gold as they flick to my hooded ice blues. He smirks.

"You abandoned us—your fated mates. What a naughty. Naughty. Girl."

He punctuates each word with a stroke of his knuckle.

The sensation on my erogenous zone morphs from pain to pleasure. My leg jerks as I mewl.

Colin grips both ankles and pulls me to the foot of the bed. I end up between his parted thighs.

My ass cheeks hang off the edge. The white silk sheets bunch about my waist. My exposed lower half draws his attention like a magnet. My hips shimmy of their own accord. His feral growl makes my pussy clench and flood with my juices. The musky scent of my arousal fills the space between us.

A predatory smile spreads across his face as his nostrils flare.

I swallow.

He grips my ankles in one sizable hand and hoists my hips from the mattress. I hang suspended with my shoulders pressed into the bed.

"Your attempt at an apology does not suffice in the least, Naughty. Naughty. Girl."

With his other hand, Colin swats my exposed pussy lips and clit.

Whap. Whap. Whap.

I howl.

The sting radiates from my core to the tips of my toes and the top of my head. An electric current of erotic punishment zaps me.

"Do you understand how much trouble you are in, Naughty. Naughty. Girl?"

When I hesitate to answer, he spanks the sensitive juncture where my thighs meet my ass.

Whap. Whap. Whap. Whap.

My legs flail as I press my hands into the mattress to drag myself away from the punishing onslaught of spanks. To no avail. Trapped.

"You can dish the pain. But not take it, Naughty. Naughty. Girl? Too bad."

Colin sets a brutal pace for my punishment. Spanks land on my clit, pussy, sit bones, and thighs. Never landing on the same spot in a row. But not in a distinguishable pattern I can expect. No matter which way I flounder, I can't avoid the blows.

My howls increase as each second passes. The time uncountable. The pain memorable.

His silence as he punishes me allows my thoughts to drift back to the many ways I hurt him, Garrett, and Dolph—my other fated mates.

Each day apart accumulates to form a mountain of unstable rocks that threaten to landslide onto me as the spanking continues unabated.

Tears stream from my eyes to pool in my ears and drip onto the bed below. Chest-racking sobs pour from my mouth. So ashamed of my actions, I cover my heated face with my hands.

My pussy, ass, and thighs on fire, I submit.

Between howls and sobs, I beg Colin for his forgiveness.

He continues to spank me.

All the tension drains from my body. Still held aloft, I sag. Spent completely. Tears continue to fall but in silence.

More time passes before the spanks change to caresses.

Soft rumblings glide over my skin as Colin soothes me. His murmurs draw more pleas of forgiveness from me. He settles on the bed and cradles me on his lap. I burrow my face into his neck as my entire body trembles. Sweat sheens on my skin, and my reddened ass is ablaze.

The punishment is a cathartic release.

"I forgive you, *My Princess*. We all do."

My heart skips a beat.

I raise my head to scan Colin's face. Can it be true?

His tawny eyes glitter in the moonlight. They're filled with what I dare hope is love. Love for me. Even after I left them without saying goodbye. Thank the gods.

His thumb brushes a tear from the corner of my eye. He slips the moistened digit past my lips.

"No more tears of sadness, *My Princess*," he murmurs before he slants his mouth over mine.

The kiss starts as a slow burn. Tendrils of warmth overtake the coldness that settled in my heart and soul. Our tongues dance an erotic tango. Flames lick through me. My toes curl as I meld my body to his muscular frame, crawling to surround him. The fire between us burns bright again.

"Need to be inside you…" Colin pants against my lips. He nips at me as he shifts position.

I lie on my back as he hovers above me. His mouth drops to my heavy breasts. He laves at the pebbled peaks. I yelp as his teeth sink into the sensitive flesh. His tongue flicks out to lap the pain away before he suckles first one, then the other distended nipple.

My head lolls. Cries of passion fall from my parted

lips. I cup the nape of his neck to encourage his ministrations. Pressed flush, he hums in pleasure. The vibrations travel through me. I mewl.

Colin stands to yank his shirt over his head. He tosses it to the floor and grips the placket of his low-slung jeans. The metal buttons pop open to reveal the swollen, purple tip of his massive cock. Commando, his erection springs free.

My mouth waters at the sight of the pearly drop of pre-cum as it glints in the moonlight. I shudder at the thought of how his turgid girth and length will burn my virgin pussy as he stretches me, forces me to take every thick inch.

He pushes the jeans past his narrow hips. The muscles in his arms and thighs flex as he wrestles the unwanted material from his body. Standing tall, he fists his cock. The veins stand out in bas-relief. His heavy sac hangs below.

My tongue darts out to lick my lower lip.

Colin smirks and jerks his cock.

My pussy gushes.

His eyes lower to the apex of my thighs. The feral smile of his wolf tips the corners of his lush mouth at the sight of my glistening pussy lips. The juices slicken my legs. He growls.

In an instant, my hips lift in the air, and my shoulders press into the bed once again. I yelp in surprise and grasp the sheets to ground myself.

Colin holds me by both ankles. Legs spread wide in a vee. My core aligned with his cock. A snap of his hips, and he impales me on his dick.

I scream from the thick invasion. His tremendous girth fills me. The burn oh so good in my tight little pussy.

"Fuck!" He roars. Head back, muscles in his neck and arms corded. Colin stills but for a moment. Then…

"Take. Every. Inch. All of it!"

He pistons balls deep within me, punctuated by each word. My only reprieve when he pulls out to his bulbous tip. Held aloft, I have no choice but to take what he gives to me. And I do with absolute pleasure.

I writhe beneath him howling like the bitch in heat I am.

Fuck, he feels so damn good…

The slapping of skin on skin with the squelch of my pussy juices mixes with his grunts and groans and my cries. The erotic sounds arouse me like no other. They spur Colin on to fuck me into the bed, drilling me into the mattress. The headboard slams against the wall, matching his rhythm.

"Oh! Oh! Yeeessss… *Colin!*" I shout as a powerful orgasm rips through me.

A flash of white light sparks behind my eyelids, squeezed shut as ecstasy rolls over me. My inner walls tighten around his pulsating cock. He growls and pummels harder. Unstoppable. Relentless.

Booms blast and bright lights explode with each of the countless orgasms Colin forces from my ravaged core.

Sweat drips from his forehead to trail between my bouncing breasts as he leans over my torso. His dominant hands wrap under me to grasp my thighs as he changes the angle of his savage thrusts. His firm pecs drag over my taut nipples. Guttural groans and growls fill my ear as Colin chases his release.

As his cock swells impossibly larger, his body judders. Hot breath puffs across my sweat-drenched neck into my damp hair.

"Sigggny…"

His carnal cry muffles as his mouth covers my exposed throat. I gasp as his elongated fangs pierce my flesh. He deepens his claiming bite with a savage growl. Copious amounts of his cum bathe my pussy and trigger another epic climax.

I scream in carnal pleasure as my eyes roll back and my back bows.

Colin's knot expands to lock behind my pelvic wall, binding us together as his seed fills my womb. We groan in unison at the added stretch. He collapses on top of me and rolls us to the side, still connected as one. The last vestiges of his release fill my core as my pussy milks his cock for every drop.

"Oh, Gods, Colin!"

My body jackknifes from the bed. A sheen of sweat coats my heated skin. My limbs tangle in the damp sheets.

I glance around, shocked to find I'm in my bedroom on Moon Island. The dream was so real, I felt every thrust of Colin's cock as though he planked above me. Not a figment of my vivid imagination.

But Colin? The one who taunted me and declared I wasn't his mate, then rescued me with tears in his eyes, refusing to let me go?

Why not Dolph, who told me from the start I am his fated mate?

Or Garrett, who acknowledged who I am to him but refuses to put me in danger by claiming me?

Perhaps Estrid's call triggered the dream and her being Colin's mother placed him as my dream lover. Whatever the reason, my empty pussy throbs, and my heavy breasts ache. For him.

Gah!

I flop back on the pillows while my body settles down.

As my eyelids flutter closed, I wonder what it all means.

Can I withstand the fated mate bond we share much longer?

COLIN

OH, Gods, Colin!

I awake to my hips pumping into the lower end of a body pillow. Serum drips down my elongated fangs embedded in the top half of pseudo-Signy. It takes a moment for the vestiges of the dream to clear. With a groan, I blow my load and sag atop the pillow.

What the *hell* was that?

I scrub a hand down my sweaty face and rest it over the erratic beat of my heart. My eyes close as I blow out a gust of air. My spent cock lies heavy between my thighs.

The dream is so damn real I smell Signy's unique scent wafting through the room, mixed with the musk of my jizz and sweat. Sex, claiming bite, knot… Only one explanation—a fated mates dream.

Fated mates often visit the other in dreams before they meet. The frequency and intensity increase the closer to them meeting in real life. A sort of bonding before the actual mate bonding ceremony occurs. In the dreams' vividness, the pair appear to be together in reality, not a dream—wet or otherwise. Sometimes they recognize one another. Often, they're not revealed, somehow shrouded or in wolf form.

I take it as the sign I need.

Time to get our fated mate.

I don't give a damn who tries to stop me.

Not even her.

"I'm coming for you, Signy. In more ways than one."

olin

"Why did you wake us at the crack of dawn?"

"Exactly. You had a nightmare you needed us to save you from?"

I growl at Dolph and Garrett.

"Actually, it wasn't a nightmare, and I damn sure didn't need saving from it," I snap.

They glance at one another, uneasy at my vicious tone. You'd be surprised how badly the loss of your mate and sexual frustration can lessen your patience. After that dream, mine has run out.

"It was a fated mate dream."

They sit straight up in their chairs. Intense gazes lock on mine. Now, I have their full attention.

"Yeah, thought you'd cut the shit talking," I say and cross my arms over my chest. "A fated mate dream so realistic, I woke to my cock jetting jizz and my fangs embedded in the pillow. Signy's sweet scent and arousal with her cries of carnal pleasure wrapping around me."

My cock hardens at the memory of spanking her round ass and taking her virginity before claiming her with my bite. I rearrange myself on the sofa to ease the throb.

"And you know what that means—"

"It's time to bring Signy back. Now," Dolph cuts in as he chops one hand onto the palm of the other.

We turn to Garrett, who sits in silence. A frown pinches his eyebrows together. Lips flatten in a stern line. He shakes his head.

"Well—"

"Oh, *hell* no!"

"I don't give a fuck whether or not you approve. It's *your* vow, not ours!"

Garrett's eyes flash cobalt with his wolf. His chest expands as a growl rumbles from deep within. He flicks his gaze between us.

Dolph and I wait, knowing the one who speaks first loses. But I narrow my eyes at Garrett and barely contain my wolf from breaking free. Anger pulsates from Dolph as he flexes his fingers, flashing golden eyes pinned on

Garrett. Good to know Dolph stands with me on this decision.

No one will stop us.

Not even our Alpha, Captain, and Commanding Officer.

"Calm the fuck down, knuckleheads," he snarls.

Dolph and I lunge at the same time. We tackle him from the chair and drag him to the floor. The bastard is strong and wrestles us. But we overpower him. Flipped onto his stomach, Dolph binds Garrett's wrists with his belt. I use mine to bind his ankles. We sit on his body as he continues to thrash. The belts won't hold a wolf shifter. But it makes our intention clear.

We vote Garrett off the island.

"For fuck's sake! Get off me! I'm with you! Let's get our fated mate. Now."

Dolph and I exchange shocked glances. Mr. Honor is going back on his word? Well, I'll be damned. We jump off, knowing he's going to swing at us once he's loose. With a grunt, he widens his arms and legs. The belts rip and fall to the floor. He flips up to a crouch, a fist on the floor, flashing eyes on us.

"Do that shit again, and we're fighting. No holds barred," he growls.

He stands and stalks towards the front door.

Dolph and I grin at each other and follow.

Ready or not, here we come, Signy.

DOLPH

AT LAST, we're taking control of this situation. Good thing Garrett let go of the whole *vow* hang up. Otherwise, we would have secured him in my safe room while we went to Miami for Signy.

The next obstacles? Jagger and Viggo, not to mention her other big brothers. But they better fall in line along with Garrett, or else we'll challenge them. And we damn sure will win. We'll burn the world down to claim our fated mate. No one will stop us from bringing Signy home to Moen Island and making her ours.

"I'm getting showered and dressed. Meet me out front in fifteen. We need to plan, and I need to ensure my father is prepared for any backlash," Garrett says when we catch up to him in the entryway.

We nod. Colin races up his stairs while I head to my mansion with a quickness.

I take the fastest shower in my life and dress in seconds. Garrett already sits in his SUV while Colin raps on the passenger door impatiently. I jog over and climb in the back. We ride in silence to Garrett's office. I stare out the window and imagine Signy's surprise when we arrive on Moon Island in a few hours.

Hopefully, the time apart ignited her instinct to accept

our bond. Allow what wolf shifters recognized since we inhabited this world to take root within the depths of her soul. Drive away her hesitancy and replace it with the primal demand to complete our bonding.

I know we're sure as hell ready.

Arne and Idonea sit in Garrett's office waiting for us. They study us as we stride inside. Arne speaks first.

"You realize Jagger will be well within his right as Alpha of the Miami Wolves Pack to challenge you should you enter his territory without permission?"

He pins each of us with an intense stare. We hold his gaze and respond at the same time.

"Yes, sir, we do."

"I expect no less, as I would do the same for Thyra."

"He better be ready to have his ass handed to him in front of his pack."

Idonea clears her throat. Our gazes swing to her.

"You have a valid reason since Signy is your fated mate. The rare occurrence supersedes all else. One highly respected with grace given to the pair—or in your case, foursome—to complete their bond no matter what. The gods made it so."

We murmur our agreement, then grow silent at her withering glare.

"But should you force Signy to leave with you or to take your claiming bite, you will answer to me. For you will not differ from the monsters who kidnapped her against her will. Am I clear?"

"And I stand by Idonea's warning. Either convince Signy to return with you or stay until she does," Arne says.

Seeing the situation the way Idonea describes it gives me pause. We are not monsters. We save females from them. Our mate will note suffer at our hands. Ever.

I pray to the gods she accepts us and returns willingly. Otherwise, we'll have no choice but to settle in Miami until we change her mind. And we will.

Garrett

"WE'RE TEN MINUTES OUT, ALPHA."

Adrenaline pumps through my veins, increasing my heart rate as the helicopter pilot's announcement travels over the sound system.

I glance at Dolph and Colin. Determination set on their faces mirror mine. We nod in full agreement on the most important mission we'll ever undertake. Operation Bring Signy Home and Claim Her.

The helicopter lowers to skim over the treetops at the center of Moon Island—the most dense area to offer us some cover. Naked except for packs on our backs holding clothes, we file to the side door and slide it open. Accustomed to working as a unit, we have no need for words once we set our plan in motion. Silently, we drop from the helicopter one after the other and land in crouches. Immediately, we shift to use our keen sense of smell to track Signy.

The balmy breeze carries the scent of jasmine and gardenias, salt from the Atlantic Ocean, and many wolf shifters in human and in wolf form. I lick my nose to increase my ability to detect Signy's unique scent.

We have only a few minutes before those in the vicinity detect us—uninvited foreign male wolf shifters. They'll attack to the death without hesitation to defend their territory.

Fortunately, my mother told us Signy lives with her parents in a bayfront mansion on the southeast side of the island. We race at full speed in that direction.

Surprisingly, we don't encounter any enforcers who undoubtedly patrol Moon Island as ours do up north. Even the scent of other wolf shifters decreases the closer we get to Signy's residence.

I don't waste time analyzing the lack of encumbrances. Instead, I count it as a blessing. The last thing I want is to fight with the Miami Wolves. That would be disastrous for our packs' relationship and for encouraging Signy to return with us.

We slow at the edge of the palm trees to scan the area. Ahead of us, a road separates the foliage from a row of mansions. As one, we tip our heads back to scent the air. A faint whiff of the forest after a spring rain, woody and earthy, with a hint of wild honey straight from the comb carries on the breeze. I pinpoint the residence on our left as the one with Signy inside. We take another glance around, then dash across the road.

Bam!

We crash into an invisible barrier. I howl in pain as my muzzle pushes back into my face. Bone crunches. Blood spews. I land on my rump. Dolph and Colin suffer the same. They stare at me with glassy eyes widened in surprise.

What the actual fuck?

Movement catches my eye.

The double front doors open.

Jagger steps out, followed by Tag, Viggo, Dylan, and Rust. They march over to the stand before us. Arms fold across their chests, feet plant far apart in dominant stances. Not a hint of surprise on their scowling faces.

I drag my glare from them when more movement happens at the door. Signy? No.

A petite, stunning female saunters over. She stands beside Jagger and places a dainty hand on his flexing biceps. Her emerald green eyes stare into my very soul. Sage—his fated mate, Luna, and the High Witch.

Of course.

Her magick alerted our presence and formed the barrier. No wonder the scent of wolves diminished the moment we arrived. She knew when we dropped from the helicopter. Hell, she probably knew we headed this way long before we arrived.

My eyes flick to the front doors in hopes Signy will emerge. Her unique scent grows stronger with them open. But she doesn't appear. I return my glare to Jagger. My eyes remain on him even as I shift back to my human form. Hastily, I yank the pack from my back and dress. Dolph and Colin do the same. We rise to our full heights.

Jagger sneers.

"You dare to enter my territory without my permission? So what? To capture my sister? I don't think so, Moen."

CHAPTER 15

igny

I ROLL over with a groan and leave the stifling confines of my Colin-less bed. I rip the damp silk camisole and panties off my hot, drenched body that still reels from the dream-induced orgasms. Then drag myself to the en suite bathroom. My jelly-like legs wobble and my empty pussy spasms from the aftereffects. I swipe the hair from my sweaty face. Strands stick to my parted lips. Panting breath blows the tendrils as my chest heaves.

With a sigh, I enter the all white Carrara marble bathroom. I bypass the extra-large claw-foot tub to opt for the walk-in shower big enough to hold four. A brief glance at the framed mirror above the double vanities reveals a flushed face and blown pupils, more aftereffects from the intense sex-not-sex. I stop in the separate water closet with a bidet and a toilet, then step into the shower.

Cool water sluices over my heated body. Massaging jets from twelve showerheads ease my stiff muscles. Eyes closed, my head tilts back for water from the rain shower-head to gently fall on my face. Finally, my body relaxes. I soothe it further with lavender bodywash. The calming scent helps the mental turmoil as my mind processes the dream and contemplates my next steps.

I can no longer deny the pull of the bond, even if it's not complete. Closing my eyes as I massage shampoo into my scalp, I can sense three threads leading from my heart to Garrett, Dolph, and Colin. Invisible lifelines link to each of them and back to me. The threads vibrate to carry their emotions straight to my heart. No pretense, even with Colin—the one who wanted nothing to do with me.

Now that I've opened my mind up to what my heart already knew, I sense their sadness, frustration, and desire. I don't need Estrid to tell me how much they miss me. The bond superhighway carries the message directly to me.

Sage's words echo in my mind, *You sense the fated mate bond. Trust the gods' choices for you.*

Trust.

That's what I will do.

Quickly, I rinse my body and hair, then hop out the

shower, drying off, and slathering lotion on my skin. I hurry to my closet more the size of a mini boutique—just call me a clothes wolf. I scan the abundant selections of casual wear, formal gowns, athleisure, party dresses, and daywear. Wanting to be comfortable for the flight up to New York, I slip into silk lingerie, an oversized cashmere v-neck sweater, and leggings. A pair of ballet flats round out my comfy outfit.

I grab my luggage and fill the pieces with sexy lingerie, footwear, and the warmest clothes I own. Although I suspect my mates will keep me naked and warm. I giggle as my cheeks heat and my pussy pulses. I prefer them wrapped around me over clothes any day!

I turn to the wall of handbags and select a few of my favorites, then place them in another piece of luggage. The roomy Bottega Veneta Cabat is the perfect bag to travel with. I put my wallet, laptop, iPad, Kindle, and a couple of paperbacks into it—the essentials.

With my toiletries bag in hand, I return to the bathroom. I fill the case with beauty products and my signature perfume. I sniff it and wonder if my mates will prefer the sensual notes of ylang-ylang and vanilla to the unique scent that defines me for them. We'll soon find out. I grin and spritz some as Coco Chanel famously said, *Wear perfume wherever you want to be kissed!*

I gather my luggage and handbag at the door. The staff will carry them to my SUV.

With my mobile in hand, I leave my wing in the

bayfront mansion I grew up in with my brothers and our parents. Jagger and Viggo moved out years ago. First to the pack's beachfront tower on Ocean Drive, where most bachelors live. Then to mansions on Moon Island after Jagger became Alpha and Viggo completed his mate bonding ceremony to Maya Alejandra Perez Garcia—his human turned wolf shifter fated mate.

Although single she-wolves live in side-by-side mansions on Moon Island under the watchful eye of Tag and the enforcers, I stayed at home. Why move into one suite when I can live in an entire wing all to myself? Of course, I redecorated my brother's suites and incorporated them into my rooms. I won't pretend. I happily wear my Miami Pack Princess crown.

It's still early. So, I head downstairs for breakfast. The tantalizing aroma of sizzling bacon, scrambled eggs, and fresh-baked biscuits makes my mouth water. I follow the scent trail to the kitchen and wave at Chef, who's busy at the Wolf range.

"Good morning, Chef! Look at all this deliciousness before me."

"Good morning, Signy. Have a seat, and I'll plate your breakfast. Everything?"

I smack my lips and rub my belly, nodding vigorously.

"Absolutely! You know me. I'm a girl who eats."

Because of wolf shifters' mega metabolism, we burn calories just sitting still. I'll enjoy a full breakfast with no concerns. Chef hooks me up, and I dive right in, exclaiming my thanks.

I scroll through my emails, text messages, and voice-mails. Nothing I need to address before I fly out. Instead, I flag them in order of importance, then set my mobile aside to finish my meal.

Only a couple of steps remain. Tell my parents about my decision to return to New York for my fated mates and ask if I may use their private jet since the crash destroyed mine. My heart clenches at the loss of our pack mates, and I say a silent prayer for their well-being.

As though sensing my thoughts, my parents appear.

"Good morning, darling."

"Good morning, sweetheart. Did you sleep well?"

A blush creeps across my cheeks as I avert my eyes. The memory of last night's erotic escapade tightens my nipples and my pussy throbs. I can only pray my parents don't detect the musky scent of my instant arousal. How embarrassing would that be?

"Oh… Good morning. I slept well, thank you," I respond as I surreptitiously press my thighs together below the banquette table. "I actually need to speak with you."

My parents exchange glances. A silent communication passes between them over their bond. My mother sits beside me while my father slides onto the opposite side. They wait for Chef to place plates in front of them and to step away before they speak.

"What's on your mind?" My father asks, studying my face.

My mother angles her body to face me, awaiting my response.

My throat works to form words. Words I hope they will understand and accept. I swallow before I speak.

"I'm going back to New York. Today. Now."

They exchange another glance, then focus on me again. I continue.

"Before, I wasn't sure I wanted to stay since I didn't have time to process all I went through"—a shudder racks my body as I recall Blaise's hands on me—"Plus, my memories returned, and I needed to reconnect with you, my brothers, and everyone else here. Although I understood Garrett, Dolph, and Colin are my fated mates and I connected with them, I wasn't certain if I could trust I would feel the same as Signy with my memories, hopes, and dreams."

I pause and implore them with my eyes.

"The time apart sparked the burgeoning bond. I need to go back. Get to know them as the total me. Let them interact with the total me. Hey, they may no longer feel a connection to this version. I just need to know if it's real."

My gaze flicks between them. They stare back expressionless as I ramble on. I suck in a breath when I finish. Their silence unnerves me. Under their intense gazes, I squirm on the leather banquette.

When they learned I had three fated mates, they

weren't pleased. At. All. My father growled and paced the living room, muttering curses. My mother's eyes widened as her jaw dropped. She asked me to repeat myself, stating she must have misheard me.

I can understand their shock and concern since I'm their baby girl, always sheltered and protected. I didn't date. No one in the pack interested me beyond friends. Plus, five older brothers and being the daughter of the Alpha deterred the males' advances. My brothers thwarted the few who attempted.

So, to go from zero to three blows my parents' minds. Even more so since multiple mates are rarer than fated mates. Now, I recall my spicy romance novels. I have my very own reverse harem. Who would expect fiction to roll off the pages into real life? The situation surprises me too.

I haven't mentioned any more about Garrett, Dolph, and Colin since I arrived. My parents probably assumed I moved on. I thought so too. But I can't. They'll have to let their baby girl fly the coop, literally.

"May I use your jet?"

My father blinks slowly. My mother opens and closes her mouth. They glance at one another. My father speaks first.

"Yours is a highly unusual situation, Signy. I understand they believe you're their fated mate. But you need more time to consider the full extent of what a pairing, uh coupling, rather group means," he says, at a loss to describe us.

I must admit it's hard to put a name on it, other than an RH. Not that my father would know anything about romance book storylines.

"I agree with your father, Signy. You've only been home for a week. That's certainly not enough time to come to such a big decision," my mother adds.

I glance between them and shake my head.

"Respectfully, I disagree. The more time passes, the more my urge to be with them increases. If I can't use your jet, I'll need to go to MIA now and get the first plane out."

"We have a problem."

My head snaps around at Jagger's voice.

He and Sage enter the kitchen. Viggo, Tag, Dylan, and Rust follow. The guys' eyebrows dip over flashing eyes. Tension radiates off them. Confused, I flick my gaze to Sage. She presses her lips together. I'm not sure if she's upset or holding back her words. I frown in return.

"What are you talking about?" I ask.

"Moen, Pihl, and Voll will be here in under fifteen minutes—"

My gasp interrupts him, but he pins me with an icy glare and continues.

"Did they contact you or vice versa?" He demands.

"No. But—"

"I thought not," he says and shifts his gaze to my father. "They're in a helicopter. I want them to get to the island. However, Sage cast an invisible barrier around this property. We'll be waiting for them to slink over here, like the sneaky dogs they are. The bastards didn't ask my permission to enter my territory. And I sure as hell won't allow them to capture Signy."

"Moen is an Alpha. He must realize the line he's crossed by just coming here uninvited. What the hell is he thinking? I wonder if Arne is aware of his son's disrespect," my father snarls.

"He's not thinking, none of them are. But they'll learn a lesson this day," Viggo growls while the others chime in with their agreement.

"Wait a minute!" I shout over them. They turn to me with scowls, as though I have no right to say anything. I glower at each of them. "No, they did not contact me. But I'm glad they're on their way. I planned to fly up to New York as soon as possible. Now, I'll fly back with them."

Silence descends. Mouths gape. Eyes widen and narrow.

"What. Did. You. Just. Say." Jagger bites out as he stomps towards me.

Trapped on the banquette seat between my parents, I can't stand easily. I glare up as he towers over me. Flashing cobalt eyes meet flashing cobalt eyes as our wolves rise to the surface. I will not back down. This is my life, my future.

"You heard me perfectly well, Jagger," I say. He growls, but I don't let him intimidate me. "I agree. They should have contacted you. But based on your behavior—barricading the house, growling like a territorial wolf, not asking me how I feel about them coming here—I don't blame them from resorting to stealth tactics. They are Green Berets after all."

"Oh, yeah? The same Green Berets who allowed their enemy to kidnap you, intending to harm you irreparably? Well, gee, perhaps I shouldn't be pissed?"

My nostrils flare at his snide comments. I stand, knocking the table.

"Hold on, Signy," my mother says as she grips my wrist and tugs me back to sit. "You can't blame your brother for looking out for you. Hear him out."

My molars grind to bite back a retort. Instead, my flashing eyes speak volumes as I glare at Jagger.

"This is my call as your Alpha. You will remain here with our parents until I deal with those three. Do you understand?"

He adds impossible to resist Alpha command to his words. The force pushes me back against the leather seat. Knowing he won't budge, I turn my gaze to Sage with the hope she'll intervene. She speaks before I can ask for her help.

"Signy, I agree with your brother. They should have spoken with him before coming here. I detected their presence shortly after they entered our pack's airspace above South Carolina," she says, then glances at Jagger. "We must not allow any wolf shifter to assume we won't defend our territory, no matter the circumstances.

However, this is unique since they are your fated mates—"

Jagger's body tenses, ready to go ballistic. But Sage places a hand on his biceps. His nostrils flare on a deep inhalation. The tension seeps out on the exhalation. Sage continues.

"I will stand by Jagger's side as Luna to our pack. But also, as Luna to you for your individual situation. I will listen to what they have to say. Then Jagger and I will decide how to proceed. Do you understand?"

"I do. However, know this, I will leave here today with my fated mates. The choice is mine and mine alone."

I look from Sage to Jagger, instilling as much steel in my tone as possible.

Sage nods. Jagger pivots on his heel.

The rest troop out.

I strain my ears to catch any sound of my mates' arrival or of Jagger's reaction. My mother reaches for my hand. I glance at her.

"You brother wants what's best for you. All of us were beside ourselves over your ordeal. You've only been home for a short period. Emotions still run high. But as you said, they are your fated mates, and it's your decision. We love you, darling, and only want you to be happy."

Tears prick the backs of my eyes. Unable to verbalize a response past the lump in my throat, I nod. I didn't imagine today going like this. I expected some pushback. But not for my brothers and my mates to fight.

What seems like hours, but is only fifteen minutes, pass before Sage returns to the kitchen. Her face doesn't reveal any reaction to what occurred. She beckons for me. My parents slide from the banquette, and I slip from the seat. My knees threaten to give out. But I steel my spine, hold my head high, and stride from the kitchen. My ears twitch to catch any sound from outside. Only a deafening silence.

My brothers stand opposite my mates. All have their arms folded across their chests as they glare at one another. Obviously, the invisible barrier remains. My heart sinks.

As one, the three of them lift their gazes to me as I walk forward. Their arms fall to their sides as their faces brighten at my appearance. They step forward, then growl in frustration at the barrier that separates us. I rush forward.

"Sage! Why is the barrier still up? I need to get to them," I declare as my palms lift to press against the invisible force. They place their palms on the other side. Our eyes lock. I gasp as the threads pulse in my heart. "Garrett. Dolph. Colin. I miss you. Take me home."

Instantly, our palms connect. I gasp at the unexpected contact. They twine our fingers and pull me in the center of them. As when they rescued me, fingers touch my face and arms., stroke my hair. Hands clutch my face. As they murmur words of love and gratitude.

"If you hurt our sister, I will hunt you down and end you with my bare hands."

Jagger's words cut into our reunion.

"Our only intention is to love, cherish, protect, and to provide for our fated mate," Garrett says as Dolph and Colin utter similar statements.

The threads sing from the joy passed along our bond.

Minutes later, we hop into my SUV, loaded with my luggage. I wave at my family with tears of gratefulness in my eyes. They wave and blow kisses. My heart swells at their acceptance of my fated mates.

At the helipad, we climb aboard their helicopter. Seated beside Dolph with Garrett and Colin opposite us, I glance out the window. Moon Island sprawls out below us. The mansions, village, and the marina slip out of view. I turn to glance back at the only home I've ever known. Then I face forward, ready for my future.

But I can't help comparing this helicopter ride to the last one. It's the complete opposite of the kidnapping where I laid on the floor, wrists bound and terrified out of my mind.

This is my choice. One I embrace fully.

Dolph slides his hand into mine. I smile up at him and turn to smile at Garrett and Dolph. They grin.

"Even though Jagger and the others didn't stop us, we would never have left without you, Signy. You are ours," Garrett says.

"And we will claim you fully once we're home on Moen Island," Dolph says.

"Yes. You are our Queen," Colin says.

The heat in his eyes makes me wonder if he felt the fated mates dream. He smirks, and I know he did.

Now, I can't wait to experience it in real life.

With all three of them.

olph

THE MUSKY SCENT of Signy's arousal blends with the forest after a spring rain, woody and earthy, with a hint of wild honey straight from the comb unique to her. As her eyes fill with hesitation, we continue to stalk towards her, closing the distance.

Once we were closer to Moen Island, Garrett told her we would claim her in the ancient way of our ancestors—run her down in wolf form. We catch her. We claim her. Forever.

She gasped. But her dilated pupils and the scent of her arousal contrasted with her shocked innocence. She shivered and sank her teeth into her plump lower lip, glancing at us from beneath the fringe of her thick eyelashes.

After the helicopter landed, Garrett told her she was to remain in human form while we shifted and to go into the forest. We gave her a head start. She flicked her eyes to each of us, then darted towards the tree line. We watched until she disappeared. As one, we shifted and threw our heads back, howling to announce the start of our claiming run.

In my mind's eyes, my wolf turned his massive head to me. With a feral glint in his eyes, he took off. Garrett and Colin's wolves raced beside mine. We caught her scent and charged after her. Howling all the way.

We caught up to her moments later. She spun around at our approach, raising her hands palms out. Her ebony black hair whipped around her. The tips brushing the top of her round ass.

"Wait! Y-You won't claim me while I'm in human form and you're wolves, will you?" She cries out in alarm.

Instinctively, a rumble rises from the depths of my chest. I want to soothe her, not have her afraid. Despite her raised hands, I pad forward and stare at her. So close, I can taste her scent on the tip of my tongue. It slips out to lick my muzzle, adding wetness to my nose to enhance her unique scent.

Ours.

Our fated mate!

We surround her.

"You won't, right?" She asks as her hands lower, cheeks flushed.

Colin's wolf snorts. His wolf won't eat her. But he will. In the most pleasurable way possible.

Distracted by her scent, I run my nose along her neck with an intense inhalation. My canines ache to issue the claiming bite as her unique scent swirls through my soul. Serum pools in my mouth.

Garrett's wolf nuzzles her ass as he rumbles.

She must sense the carnal hunger in us, and she sidesteps away. We follow with more rumbling. She will not deny us. In her haste, she trips over a rock and lands on that luscious ass. I hold back a snicker as her eyes stretch in shock.

Instead, I take advantage of her position and tower above her much smaller form before I return my muzzle to her throat, once again tempted to bite. When she mewls, I almost lose control. My nose trails down her body to the source of her arousal as it mixes with her scent. I press against her pussy through the leggings. An irritated growl slips past my lips at the encumbrance of her clothes. I want her bare to us. Now.

I force my wolf back to the edges of my being and shift. Flashes flare around us as Colin and Garrett shift as well.

"Ours!" We growl in unison.

With a smirk, I grab the offensive sweater and rip it to pieces. The silky bra follows. Delicious full tits with beaded rosy nipples appear before my hooded eyes. My mouth waters to savor them. But her whimper catches my attention. Her sweet cry drives me over the edge.

I lower my lips to her tits. My tongue laps at the soft underside curve of one before it licks a trail to the nipple. Her back arches, bringing her tit closer to my face as I wrap my tongue around the tip, savoring her tantalizing taste. My cock bobs against my eight-pack abs, the bulbous tip slick with pre-cum reaches my navel. My cock throbs to join the action as I feast on her tits. I ignore it, focused on her pleasure.

Garrett growls. My eyes lift to find him capture her mouth for a spine-tingling kiss. She mewls as his tongue dominates hers as he demands she give him access to all of her. A nudge to my flank from Colin moves me to her side. My mouth never leaves her tits. He yanks her leggings off and lowers his mouth to her cunt. The three of us groan in unison as her musky arousal wafts from her needy pussy.

Her head jerks from Garrett. A long moan slips past her swollen lips as Colin devours her pussy. His grunts of satisfaction make me greedy for some of her honey. His hands wrap around her hips for his fingers to dig into her thighs, parting them for more access. She bucks and cries out from his carnal onslaught.

The vibrations from my chest as I soothe her with more rumbling shoot through my body, adding fuel to an already smoldering core.

More of her soft cries slip past Garrett's mouth as she writhes beneath us prove to be my undoing. I must have her. But first, more of those succulent tits. The rough flatness of my tongue and sharp bites to her sensitive skin makes her yelp. I rumble. My tongue winds around her nipple. I suckle on the tip, savoring her sweet flavor. My mouth widens to encompass more of her pillowy tit. Delicious.

My wolf joins in on my feral cries as we make a meal of her tits, going from one to the other. She continues to writhe and moan. She returns my bites with those from her fingernails as she clings to me. Her unique scent merges with the musky arousal coming from her pussy as Colin eats her raw like the wild beast he is.

The tip of my cock springs forth more pre-cum, eager to drive inside as I mount her. But again, I delay my satisfaction to get her as ready for my length and girth as possible. She's so much smaller than us. Our fated mate is bound to have a tight little pussy. And she's a virgin. I don't want to cause unintentional pain.

I ghost my lips over her concave belly, then trail open-mouthed kisses back up to her heaving chest. A husky groan falls from my mouth as I close in on my prize. I nuzzle her tits with the tip of my nose before my tongue demands in on the action. I swipe it from her areole to her nipple that's as hard as my dick.

Colin growls. She throws her head back and screams.

Her back arches as her hips rise from the ground, pushing her sweet pussy further into his hungry mouth.

Garrett and I watch as Colin smirks against her pussy lips. I think of her howl when I thrust inside of her tight, wet heat. And her pussy is tight. So tight it clamps onto my cock as I spear it inside. The vision flickers before my eyes.

Damn if she isn't super responsive to our touch.

As she bucks from his unrelenting feasting, he slides his hands around her narrow hips and holds her ass to still her movements. He wants her to focus on the pleasurable sensations his mouth has on her pussy and on how much better our dicks will feel buried inside.

It doesn't take long for her to come undone for us. Once again, her screams rock the forest. As her body shakes uncontrollably, her fingers grip the long strands of Colin's hair. He grunts from the pain.

"Now, we make you ours!" He declares as he sits back on his haunches with a stare so hot, she shudders and gasps.

A split second later, she leaps to her feet and runs.

⸰⸱

SIGNY

. . .

MY HEART POUNDS as I run as fast as my wobbly legs can carry me. Wild thoughts run through my mind as I think of what just happened.

Their hands and mouths were everywhere on me, causing me to erupt like a volcano. Heat engulfed my body and poured from deep within my core as I quaked with each pulse.

My knees wobble at the memory, and I lose my footing. But I don't stop. However, I risk a glance over my shoulder. A shiver runs through me at the sight of the sexy beasts loping after me.

Their eyes flash as animalistic growls pour from their mouths. They fan out around me, hunting me like a wild pack of wolves. Their predatory behavior shoots a bolt of desire through my core.

My pussy clenches as more liquid slips down my slick inner thighs, still coated with the remnants of my eruption. I stumble as one throws his head back and howls, another roars, and the last snarls. A cry slips past my lips, even as I ache for their touch.

I dart further into the forest, hoping to put distance between us. My wolf runs with me, excited by the chase. The beasts howl and pursue me. Wildlings in pursuit of their prey. I dodge fallen trees and push through bushes as I zigzag my way in a random pattern.

They're taunting me. They could catch me at anytime they choose. Their much longer and muscular legs can easily outrun me. However, they're enjoying the chase too much for a quick catch. I shudder, thinking what will happen once they get their hands on me again.

I thought we'd take time to reconnect. I didn't expect to be chased down and claimed as soon as we arrived. But I can't say I'm mad about it. My heart pounds in my chest and my pussy throbs.

A cabin stands ahead. I burst past the tree line. Perfect! I can lock myself inside. Although I doubt the door would keep the giants out. But the thought flies from my mind as a body collides with mine.

It knocks the air from my lungs as I squeal in surprise. Strong arms bind around my torso, pinning my arms to my sides. The body twists and lands on its back with me on top, my back to its front. With a cock the size of an anaconda wedged between us, I land on my captor with a grunt. Then my lower arms and legs flail.

"That's far enough, mate."

Warm breath caresses my sweat-dampened cheek as Colin murmurs against the shell of my ear. His intoxicating scent engulfs me—spices, leather, and musk—depleting me of any resistance. Again. He rumbles, and I sag as the vibrations roll through every cell of my heated body. A mewl escapes my parted lips.

"Don't be frightened, little one."

"We caught you. We've proven we're strong enough to claim you."

My hooded eyes raise to Garrett and Dolph. Passion burns on their handsome faces. Chiseled cheekbones, firm jaws dusted with stubble, lush mouths. Mouths that did unimaginable things to my body. A tremble courses through me, only to turn into a full-body shudder when the cock nestled between me and the other pulsates. Colin chuckles beneath me.

His hands slip from my torso to my hips, where he squeezes them. I yelp at the unexpected touch. He rumbles as he sits up, bringing me with him to settle me on his lap. His lips brush the side of my face before it lowers to the juncture where my neck meets shoulder. His teeth scrape the sensitive area. My eyes flutter close on a groan as my head lolls to the side, granting him better access. He growls and nips, then rumbles when I cry out.

"It's all right, sweetheart. We'll prepare you for our claiming bite."

My eyes pop open as the word bite rips through the carnal haze. I gasp and wiggle to free myself from Colin's lap. But he tightens his grip on my hips and rumbles deep in his chest. I mutter a curse as the sound soothes my instinct to run.

My gaze flicks to Garrett crouching before me. I force my eyes to remain on his face and not travel down the ridges of his muscles to the giant cock I see in my periphery. I take a fortifying breath.

"*Signy.*"

My name murmured on their lips sounds so erotic, my pussy spasms gushing more liquid onto my inner thighs. It drips along the curve of my ass and onto Colin's lap. He groans and rocks his hips. His cock thumps against my back. I mewl and grind against him, unable to stop my reaction.

Their eyes close as they inhale deeply and groan as one. They open their eyes and pin me with intense stares.

"We are fated mates. You are ours," Garrett says as his eyes flash cobalt blue.

His possessive tone shoots sparks in my pussy. It swells and gushes. He smirks as he stares back at me with heavy-lidded eyes full of lust.

Dolph's eyes smolder. I have no doubt Colin's do too, as his grip on my hips tightens on a low growl.

"Time to make your ours, Queen," he rasps as he lifts me from his lap and stretches me out on a bed of pine needles.

They kneel around me. Three hulking males. I distinguish each one as my eyes move from one gorgeous face to the other. Colin with serious eyes. Garrett's open. Dolph with a twinkle in his. Determination sets in their features. A moan slips past the lips on my face even as the lower ones swell with a desperate, aching need.

I've never felt a pull so strong.

An animalistic growl draws my attention to Colin. He bares his elongated fangs as he stares at my heaving chest. The other two follow with hungry growls of their own. Their frames grow larger as muscles thicken. I gasp at their ferociousness. They lift their heated gazes to pin me with intense otherworldly stares.

My pussy clenches. I mewl.

A rumble vibrates in the air and wraps around me. But a snarl from Dolph breaks the hold. My wide eyes swivel to him. Fists clench at his sides. The snarl continues past his curled upper lip as his eyes penetrate my soul. He leans forward at my soft cry. But he sways back and shakes his head, holding me captive with his glowing eyes. He chuckles wickedly.

The rumble returns to rouse me from his hypnotic gaze. Instinctively, my body relaxes as the comforting sound drowns out the chuckle. I stare up at Colin.

He glances down at my bare leg, then places one finger on the inside of my ankle. As he trails the tip along my instep, I moan aloud. All thoughts slip away, replaced by carnal desire.

"We've waited too long for you," he murmurs.

I gasp at the pressure he applies with his knuckle to the sole of my foot.

His eyes flick to my hooded ice blue eyes, now darkened to cobalt with desire. He smirks.

"You captivate us more than you can imagine."

He punctuates each word with a stroke of his knuckle.

The sensation on my erogenous zone morphs from pain to pleasure. My leg jerks as I mewl.

Garrett grips my other ankle. Together, they lift my legs in the air. I end up between their muscular thighs. They flex against my hips.

My exposed pussy draws their attention like a magnet.

My hips shimmy of their own accord. Feral growls make my pussy clench and flood with more liquid. The musky scent of my arousal mingles with their spices, leather, and musk.

Predatory smiles spread across their faces as their nostrils flare. Their heads tip back as they inhale deeply, eyes squeeze shut. Dolph leans forward and cups my ass.

I swallow.

Suddenly, their grips tighten on my ankles in their sizable hands. In one seamless motion, they hoist my hips from the pine needles. I hang suspended with my shoulders pressed into the ground. My pussy leaks liquid down my thighs to the curve of my ass before it drips beneath me. My hands cover my reddened face as I groan. A mixture of carnal lust and embarrassment runs through my heated body.

"Do not hide from us, little one."

Firm fingers grip my wrists and pull my hands from my face. I stare up into the face of Dolph. His warm breath sweeps over my skin, leaving goose bumps in its wake. He lowers his full lips to my throat. Nips and sucks my pebbled nipples even as my pussy gushes more. He chuckles against my sensitive skin.

"You smell so sweet."

I mewl as I lengthen my neck to give him better access. He growls appreciatively.

"Never leave us again, Queen."

Hands swat my exposed pussy lips and clit.

Whap. Whap. Whap. Whap.

I howl.

The sting radiates from my core to the tips of my toes and to the top of my head. An electric current of erotic punishment zaps me.

"Do you understand how much we missed you?"

"How we ached for you?"

When I hesitate to answer, they spank the sensitive juncture where my thighs meet my ass.

Whap. Whap. Whap. Whap.

My legs flail as I press my hands into the ground to drag myself away from the punishing tattoo of spanks. To no avail. Trapped by Dolph's arms banded around my shoulders.

"Embrace the pain before the pleasure," he murmurs against the shell of my ear, then chuckles as I shiver. "I promise, we'll make you cum so hard, you'll see stars."

The pair of burly males set a brutal pace. Spanks land on my clit, pussy, sit bones, and thighs. Never landing on the same spot in a row. But not in a distinguishable pattern I can expect. No matter which way I flounder, I can't avoid the blows as Dolph pins me in place. Open-mouthed kisses trail along my collarbones and neck. He brushes his lips over mine. A satisfied groan rumbles in the back of his throat.

My howls increase as each second passes. The time uncountable. The pain unforgettable.

Tears stream from my eyes to pool in my ears and drip

onto the pine needles below. Chest-racking sobs pour from my slack mouth.

My pussy, ass, and thighs on fire, I submit to their dominance.

Between howls and sobs, I beg them to forgive me.

They continue to spank me.

All the tension drains from my body. Still held aloft, I sag. Spent completely. Tears continue to fall but in silence.

The spanks switch to caresses.

Soft rumblings glide over my skin as all three males soothe me. Their murmurs draw more pleas of forgiveness from me. They lower me onto the pine needles. Dolph slides me along until my head rests on his lap. He strokes my wet cheeks. The other two bracket my body. I burrow my face into Dolph's thigh as my entire body trembles. Sweat sheens on my skin, and my reddened ass blazes.

His thick, long dick bulges beneath my cheek. My mouth waters. I turn my head and nuzzle him. His hard cock jumps. I moan, wanting to taste him.

"You will not leave us ever again, will you?"

My heart skips a beat at Colin's raspy voice.

I raise my head to scan his face.

His eyes glitter like golden.

His thumb brushes along my inner thigh. He glides the digit on the wet trail of my pussy liquid. My hips buck as I mewl.

"No, never."

A feral grin spreads across his face.

"Good girl."

I bite my lower lip at his praise. But a possessive growl from Garrett draws my attention to him.

He holds my gaze as he lowers his mouth to my other thigh. Instead of his thumb, he uses the flat of his tongue to lap at the wet trails all the way to my throbbing core. When he swipes from my puckered hole, past my swollen pussy lips, and up to wrap around my engorged clit, I jackknife from Dolph's lap. I keen as an unexpected orgasm races through me.

"So sweet," he murmurs against my gushing pussy. "I'm going to eat you up."

He makes good on his promise as he devours my dripping pussy. With each gush, his growls increase in ferocity. Tongue lashes my puffy, slick lower lips, sopping up every drop. Teeth nip at the sensitive bundle of nerves. I squeal as more liquid spurts into his hungry mouth. My entire body quivers as he groans in male erotic pleasure.

Dolph growls before he slams his mouth over mine, swallowing my passionate cries. The dominating kiss sends tendrils of warmth straight into my heart and soul. Our tongues dance an erotic tango. Flames lick through me. My toes curl as I mold my body to his muscular frame. My hands scrabble along his muscular chest to bring him even closer. The fire between us burns hot.

"Need to be inside you..." Colin growls. Dolph nips at me as he shifts position and grasps my wrists in one sizable hand. He presses them against the ground above my head.

I lie on my back as my three mates hover above me. Mouths drop to my heavy breasts. Tongues lick at the pebbled nipples. I yelp as teeth sink into the sensitive flesh. Tongues flick out to lap the erotic pain away before they suckle each one of my distended nipples.

My head lolls. Cries of passion fall from my parted lips. Pressed flush to my breasts, they hum in pleasure. The vibrations travel through me. I mewl, then my eyes widen as Colin kneels between my spread thighs and fists his erection. The veins stand out in bas-relief. His heavy sac hangs below. The muscles in his arms and thighs flex as he glides his fist along the thick shaft to the tip.

My mouth waters at the sight of the pearly drop at the slit. I shudder at the realization his turgid girth and length will burn as he thrusts into my little pussy and stretches me to accommodate his colossal size.

My tongue darts out to lick my lower lip.

He smirks and jerks his cock.

My pussy gushes.

His eyes lower to the apex of my thighs. A carnal smile tips the corners of his lush mouth at the sight of my glistening pussy lips. The liquid slickens my legs. He growls.

In an instant, my hips lift in the air, and my shoulders press into the Dolph's lap once again. I yelp in surprise. But he and Garrett hold me firm.

Colin holds me by both ankles. Legs spread wide in a

vee. My core aligns with his cock. A snap of his hips, and he impales me on his dick.

I scream from the thick invasion as it tears through my virginity. His tremendous girth fills me. The burn oh so good.

"I'm your first!" He roars. Head back, muscles in his neck and arms corded. He stills but for a moment. Then...

"Take. Every. Inch. All of it!"

He pistons balls deep within me, punctuated by each word. My only reprieve when he pulls out to his bulbous tip. His eyes flash as he stares at the blood coating his cock. His nostrils flare. Garrett and Dolph sniff the air and groan. They bury their faces against my breasts.

Held aloft, I have no choice but to take what Colin gives to me as he continues to plow into my virgin pussy. And I take it with absolute pleasure.

I writhe beneath him howling like the bitch in heat I am.

Gods, he feels so damn good...

The slapping of skin on skin with the squelch of my pussy juices mixes with his grunts and groans and my cries. The erotic chorus arouses me like no other symphony. They spur him on to fuck me into the ground.

"Oh... Oh... Yeeessss!" I shout as a powerful orgasm rips through me.

A flash of white light sparks—stars as Dolph promised—behind my eyelids, squeezed shut as ecstasy rolls over me. My inner walls tighten around his pulsating cock. He growls and pummels harder. Unstoppable. Relentless.

Garrett and Dolph join in his feral beast-like groans while mine mix in for an erotic composition.

Booms blast and bright lights explode with each of the countless orgasms he forces from my ravaged core.

Sweat drips from his forehead to trail between my bouncing breasts as he leans over my torso. Garrett and Dolph move aside, stroking my arms. Colin's dominant hands wrap under me to grasp my thighs as he changes the angle of his savage thrusts. His firm pecs drag over my taut nipples. Guttural groans and growls fill my ear as he chases his release.

As his cock swells impossibly larger, the base thickens to lock behind my pelvic wall. His body judders. Hot breath puffs across my sweat-drenched neck into my damp hair.

"Mine!"

His carnal cry and the copious amounts of his cum bathing my pussy trigger another epic climax.

I scream in pleasure as my eyes roll back and my back bows.

He collapses on top of me. I bear his heavy weight happily. The last vestiges of his release drip from my core, down my ass cheeks to the drenched pine needles below.

I scream as pain laces around my throat. He growls as his teeth bury deeper into my flesh. Garrett and Dolph hold my arms out to the sides, preventing me from breaking free. They growl and snarl like wild animals. Hot saliva drips from inhumanly long teeth onto my bare arms. I cry out in alarm even as my pussy clamps around his cock, milking him of his seed.

"Mine!"

"Mine!"

Garrett and Dolph chorus in savage voices with nostrils flared before they lower their mouths to my neck as Colin lifts his face and stares down at me. His cock still buried deep in my pussy.

"You are now ours, Signy Moen Pihl Voll."

My mouth opens in a silent scream.

Darkness descends.

COLIN

"IT'S BEEN a while since we shared a she-wolf in the cabin."

"Yeah, but this time, she's our fated mate. No one else will ever share our bed."

I listen to Garrett and Dolph as I carry a sleeping and naked Signy through the cabin's door.

The cabin is rugged. A great room with furniture and the kitchen with a dining table. One bedroom with a massive bed and a bathroom.

"We'll wait until she awakes before we take her home. We'll shift to wolf form to get back quickly," Garrett says.

I stretch Signy out on the bed after Garrett pulls the quilt down. She murmurs in her sleep, then rolls to her side as I rumble to soothe her and place the quilt over her body. We pile onto the bed, surrounding her with our bodies.

My heart swells with joy at claiming our fated mate. Our virgin fated mate, who will know no other males but us. My dick swells along with my heart as I remember pushing past her innocence, her pussy gripping me like a vise, and pumping her to overflowing with my seed. I grin, imagining her belly round with one of our pups. Hell, it was better than the dream.

"Don't gloat because you had her first, fucker."

Dolph's words draw me back to the bedroom.

"This time, I have to agree fully with Dolph," Garrett adds, then cuts his eyes to Dolph. "But I'll let it slide since we'll go in rank order."

He growls.

"Fuck both of you!"

Garrett and I glance at each other and laugh, albeit quietly, so as not to awaken Signy.

Dolph grumbles and shakes his head as he returns his gaze to her.

∿

DOLPH

HOURS LATER, Signy stirs.

The three of us sit up. We hover around her, waiting for her eyes to open. When they do, it's as if the gods sing.

Vibrant ice blue irises stare at us, then widen in her beautiful heart-shaped face. She gasps and sits up. Her silky, jet black hair cascades down her back and over her tits. But the thick mane can't hide her nipples as they poke through the strands. The nipples tighten with her arousal as her musky scent fills the room.

My cock tents the quilt. I bite back a groan.

"I—I wasn't dreaming?" Her wide eyes flick from one of us to the other as her hands lift to her neck. Her fingertips brush over our claiming bites, and she winces. "It *is* real…"

"No, it wasn't a dream," Garrett says and leans towards her neck. "I'll make the pain less."

He laps at the bites to use his saliva to increase the healing process. I want to be jealous. But I'm not. Had he been another male, I would have clawed his tongue from his mouth and shoved it up his ass.

Colin shoots me a side glance.

I wave him off.

"Are you thirsty?" I ask ready to give her a bottle of water from the kitchen. I'll do anything for our fated mate.

Her eyes slide to me, and I smile.

"Yes, please."

I leave the room and return with the water. I uncap the bottle and hold it to her lips.

Her eyebrows dip. But I shake my head. She will drink from my hand. No need for her to hold the bottle. I will hand feed her too when we return to Garrett's mansion. It's the dominant in me that wants to tend to her needs. I smile as she places her full lips on the bottle's rim, and I tilt it, careful not to spill it on her.

"Thank you," she says after she drinks her fill.

I nod as pride warms my chest.

"How do you feel?" Colin asks as he steps closer.

Her eyes leave mine as she turns to him. A blush tints her cheeks.

"Uh… A bit sore. But, um, fine otherwise," she murmurs as more color stains her cheeks red. She shifts on the bed and draws the quilt over her tits.

"I'll lick it better for you."

The words slip from my mouth instead of remaining in my head as I intended.

She gasps and covers her face with her hands. Her shoulders shake.

"Dammit, Dolph!"

"You upset her, fucker!"

My heart sinks.

"Signy, I—"

"No. No," she cuts in as she lowers her hands. Her eyes

dance with mirth as she looks at me. "I'm not upset. That was funny, Dolph!"

I sag in relief, dropping to the bed and pulling her into my arms. She cuddles against my chest, wrapping her arms around my waist. She giggles, and we join in.

Garrett

MY HEART SINGS with Signy's laughter. Thank the gods Dolph didn't make her cry. I would've clocked him upside his head.

I watch him hold her as I think about how great it is to claim our fated mate. Not just mine, but one for the three of us to share.

She takes each of our hands and places them one on top of the other over her heart. It beats in a steady rhythm. A smile spreads across her face, shining in her eyes.

"Do you feel our bond? The threads solid now?" She asks.

"Yes," we respond emphatically.

"Good. Now, take me home with you. I'm ready to be your Queen. Forever."

CHAPTER 17

igny

TINGLES FLOW through my body as I relive my mates claiming me. From the breathless run to the cathartic spanking to Colin's first thrust ripping through my virginity followed by their fangs embedded in my flesh, I quiver with desire.

Sage and my other sisters-in-law shared bits about of their claiming. But they never mentioned the claiming run. I've heard elder she-wolves reminisce about their experiences and the thrill of being chased and claimed by their feral mates in the most primal way.

I must admit I prefer the savagery. My wolf grins with her tongue lolling. She drops to her back, baring her belly in complete submission. I chuckle at the brazen hussy.

"What's so funny, Baby Girl?"

I glance up at Dolph, color reddening my heated cheeks. He quirks an eyebrow and sniffs. A predatory grin spreads across his face. He scents my arousal. Naked since they ripped up my clothes, I shuffle from one foot to the next. My movements enhance the musky scent wafting in the surrounding air.

He growls deep in his chest and presses a possessive kiss to his claiming bite as a long, thick finger plunges into my leaking pussy. He curls and twists the digit to stroke my G-spot. The other hand grips my hip to keep me in place.

I mewl and dig crescents into his bare forearms as my fingers cling to him. He adds another finger and pumps them in and out, fucking me onto my toes. His savage growls fill my ear as he presses his mouth to my throat. He nips and laves the bare skin.

A firm chest presses against my back. Muscular thighs mold against the backs of my legs as a pelvis cradles my ass. The long, thick cock wedges its hard shaft between my cheeks. Sizable hands cup my breasts. The calloused fingers pinch and tug my peaked nipples.

"You think we'll let Dolph dominate all of your pleasure?"

Colin's gruff voice fills my other ear.

I shudder and cry out as Dolph incites a toe-curling

orgasm. Pussy juices gush into his hand. He groans and drops to his knees. His hot mouth covers my slick folds. The flat of his tongue laves the abundant juices. Vibrations from his feral growls travel across my sensitive pussy. More cries pour from my mouth.

"Absolutely not," Garrett rumbles before his mouth crashes onto mine. His tongue thrusts inside and licks every inch of my mouth. "You're ours to share."

I gasp as my knees buckle. I'm dizzy from their erotic onslaught. Brain misfires. Limbs twitch. Heart stutters. A series of orgasms hit me one after the other, unending carnal pleasure. I quiver from head to toe.

"Oh, *gods!*"

They push me to the ground on my knees and rise to tower above me. Through half-mast eyes, I tilt my head back to see them. Faces twist with agony. Eyes narrow. Nostrils flare. Lips twist. Their biceps flex as veins stand out on their forearms. Fists pump their ginormous cocks.

"Open your mouth," Colin barks through clenched teeth.

Immediately, I obey, eyes trained on him.

He groans at my submission and places the tip of his cock on my bottom lip. His shoulders hunch. Cords stick out on his neck. His head falls back. He roars as thick ropes of his hot, creamy seed jettison from his cock to fill my mouth. Despite me doing my best to swallow his cum, the excess dribbles down my chin.

A fist lifting my hair and a groan from behind me are

all the warnings I receive before a hot stream of cum splashes onto my back.

"Fuck!" Dolph growls.

"Head back. Eyes on me," Garrett commands.

Again, I don't hesitate. My heavy breasts jut out. Furled nipples point to the sky. Eyes lock on Garrett's feral eyes. He sucks in a breath.

"Fffuuuck…"

His hot cum coats my breasts. Pearlescent beads dangle from the tips of my nipples. His hands reach out to rub his cum into my skin. Possessive eyes rove over me, tightening my nipples further. My empty pussy clenches, greedy to be filled by their seed.

"Swallow it all," Colin says as his thumb scoops his cum from my chin to my mouth. Eyes blaze when I suck the digit clean.

Dolph's hands move in circles on my back.

"We mark you with our scent for all males to know you are *ours*," he growls.

"Only ours," Colin adds, eyes flashing with his wolf.

"No one else will ever touch you," Garrett says and sniffs the air. "Now, we take you home. Shift."

As only an Alpha can command, the three of us shift. Garrett stares at each of our wolves, then nods and shifts into his massive jet black wolf. He barks and takes off. We follow with yips and barks.

As we race through the forest, I observe the terrain. Less snow covers the ground, exposing the dried grass and underbrush. Twigs crunch beneath our paws. We leap over boulders and dart between trees. Early evening sunlight dapples the ground and glistens on the water of a stream. We splash across. Birds take flight while other creatures scurry away from the path of four predators.

I wonder if the pack runs as one through the forest as Miami does through the Everglades. Based on what I saw from the helicopter, the island is more than large enough to accommodate pack runs. I imagine how beautiful it must be in the spring and summer months. The deciduous trees stand full of green leaves. Colorful wildflowers grow in abundance. A carpet of fresh grass spread across the ground.

The fall season is an explosion of vibrant reds, golds, and oranges as the famous New York fall foliage transforms the landscape. A colorful picture book come to life.

I experienced enough of winter. I can't wait for the other seasons. And for buying new clothes for them. Which makes me wonder if the house has enough closet space. Which leads to, whose house will we live in for our foursome?

As I ponder the possibilities, my nose detects wolf shifters in human and wolf forms nearby. Their scents mix with the smoke of oak logs from chimneys and various meats and food cooking for dinner. Children's laughter and adults' conversations carry on the breeze.

I glance around and notice backyards of impressive mansions abut the forest. Straight ahead streetlights glow as the sun sets. The sound of a motorcycle engine roars as it goes by on the road.

Garrett barks and darts to the left. We avoid the road and race behind the mansions. Further on, we approach the rear of a larger mansion. He veers towards the flagstone patio with a swimming pool surrounded by chaise lounges and outdoor kitchen and living room. He pauses at a side door.

A dramatic carving of a wolf etched in the wood welcomes us. Garrett slaps his paw on a panel, and the door swings open. He lopes inside. Dolph's wolf nudges me forward with his muzzle against my flank, and I enter. He and Colin follow. The door swings closed.

Garrett shifts. My tongue lolls at the sight of his golden skin with tattoos stretched over chiseled muscles. His massive dick—even flaccid—hangs like a pendulum between his thighs. He senses me drooling and winks as he slips into a pair of black joggers. They sit low on his hips to reveal the lickable V-cuts of his Adonis belt.

"Like what you see, Our Queen?"

I shift.

"Absolutely, my Alpha," I purr with hooded eyes. My fingertips trail over his defined pecs. I tweak his nipple.

He growls and grips me on the back of my neck. He yanks me flush to him and slants his mouth over mine. Greedy to possess all of me, he swallows my lusty moans. My fingers tangle in his long, jet black hair. He grunts when I tug the silky strands. I whimper at a nip to my lower lip and a sharp crack on my ass.

"You need to eat, and we need to discuss a few things," he says, zoned in on my swollen lips, reluctant to end our kiss.

Dolph and Colin stalk past us, also in joggers. I watch their toned asses flex beneath the thin cotton. Yum.

I yelp as another spank to my ass jolts me onto my toes.

"Get moving," Garrett commands.

I glance at the wardrobe they removed the joggers from. I reach for a t-shirt, then yelp again. My head snaps to Garrett. I arch an indignant eyebrow.

"When you're home, you wear nothing. We want you bare and available to us at all times," he says with a raised eyebrow of his own.

My eyes widen.

"What?"

He shakes his head and tosses me over his shoulder as though I weigh nothing. He smacks my ass and holds his palm over the stinging flesh.

"No. Clothes. Naked."

He issues three more spanks for each word.

I growl and shimmy my hips to avoid the blows. He growls deeper and issues a harder spank.

"Be still and accept," he growls.

Even though my mind revolts, my pussy drips my arousal onto his shoulder. He chuckles wickedly and pats my ass. He strides into the kitchen where the aroma of steaks sizzling on the grill fills the air.

"Figured I'd get dinner going since you two were delayed," Dolph says dryly.

Garrett lowers me into his arms and sits at the over-sized marble island. He positions me on his lap with my back to his chest and my thighs spread gripping the outsides of his legs. He wraps his arms around my waist and holds me close, his chin on my shoulder.

I sigh and settle against him.

Colin pours cabernet sauvignon into three crystal wineglasses and doles them out. Garrett tips his glass to my lips. I sip the robust wine as Colin drops onto the chair beside us. With a smirk, he pinches my nipple.

I yelp and squirm, even as my pussy clenches. The scent of my arousal mingles with the steaks' aroma.

"You smell as tantalizing as these Kobe sirloins. I'm sure that delicious ass of yours is as marbled as the steak after Garrett spanked you," Dolph snickers.

My cheeks heat, and I hang my head.

Colin places his index finger under my chin and lifts, turning my head until our eyes align.

"We are your fated mates. Never be embarrassed with us. We will never say or do anything to shame you. You are Our Queen."

Dolph and Garrett agree. Each one kisses me until I'm breathless.

Once the steaks are ready, Garrett keeps me on his lap

while they hand feed me delectable morsels until my belly protests. He carries me to the living room. Colin fills three crystal tumblers with Macallan whisky and hands them out. He pulls me onto his lap and lifts his tumbler to my mouth. The straight whisky burns as it cascades down my throat. It lights a fire in my belly. I lick my lips for more. Colin grins and complies.

Dolph settles on the sofa beside us while Garrett sits on the matching leather ottoman. He clears his throat.

"We have separate residences with mine being this one, flanked by Dolph and Colin's. As Alpha and Luna, you will be here," he says and flicks his gaze at the other two. "These crybabies don't want to sleep without you."

I giggle and pat their cheeks. They shrug, unrepentant.

"We ordered a custom giant bed to accommodate us comfortably, along with a few other items. All will arrive in a few days and replace my existing bed. Until then, we'll pile into my California king."

My stomach twists at the vision of Garrett fucking other females in his bed. Their cries as they writhe beneath him ring in my ears. My arms wrap around my middle protectively as I struggle to move beyond the pain that lances my heart.

"Hold on, Signy," Garrett growls as he pulls me from Colin to straddle his lap.

My head dips, making my hair fall like a curtain to hide the emotions rolling across my face.

"Look at me," he commands.

I lift my gaze to stare at his forehead.

"Un-uh. Eyes on me."

My gaze lowers to his eyes. He pins me with an intense stare.

"No other female has been in my bed. Not even in my house other than my mother, Thyra, and Vera—my brother Randel's mate. Only you, Signy."

Relief courses through me, dissipating the images. I close my eyes and lean my forehead against his as he rumbles deep in his chest to soothe me. Our breaths mingle. I sigh and wrap my arms around his neck. Hands stroke my back as Dolph and Colin murmur words of love. Their intoxicating scents cocoon me.

"We can also change one of the guest suites into a retreat space for you. In fact, you can redecorate all our houses if you prefer a fresh look."

Dolph nods and adds, "We want you to make our homes yours too. Do whatever you want."

Colin nods.

"Actually, this house is so large, I'm sure I can find a room to escape your ravishing touches," I say with a grin. They grumble, and I continue. "However, I will accept your offer to redo a guest suite. I need to recreate my closet. Especially given I'll need new clothes for the different seasons."

They snort and mumble about females and clothes and me not needing any inside the house. But Garrett agrees, and they give me free rein over their—rather, *our*—homes.

I sit up more seriously. They quiet down.

"The reason I flew to New York all those weeks ago was to visit Fashion Week to select items for my new business. I'm launching a luxury online boutique, Signy's Secret Cache. I plan to continue my dream. Since it's online, I can run it anywhere."

Dolph cups my cheek.

"We will never stop you from accomplishing your dreams or control you in any way—"

"Aside from in the bedroom," Colin cuts in.

They nod in unison.

I giggle and shake my head. These males!

"Another thing," I say.

Three sets of eyes focus on me.

"I've always dreamed of my mate bonding ceremony being fit for a princess. A grand affair with my and my mate's packs along with those from the other territories—"

"You will have all your heart desires, Signy," Garrett says, placing a finger against my lips to silence me. "We will give you all that you want and so much more. Let us show you the life you'll have with us, Our Queen, starting with our seclusion."

He rises and carries me up the stairs to his bedroom suite.

For the rest of the night and Yhe next seven days, my fated mates give me their all with no interruptions.

And I happily give them mine.

CHAPTER 18

olin

"THAT'S A GOOD GIRL, pet. Embrace the erotic pain and the pleasure will increase tenfold," I murmur in her ear.

My tongue trails from the delicate shell along her sweat-dampened jaw and dips between her parted lips. She gasps. I lick the inside of her mouth, tasting every inch before tangling her tongue with mine for a dominant kiss. She moans, followed by a grunt. I swallow both.

Dolph wields the flogger with practiced precision to slap the suede tails against her reddened ass. Cuffed by her wrists and her ankles to the St. Andrew's Cross, she accepts her Dom's strokes like a good little sub. Her breathy moans combined with the scent of her arousal confirm her body knows what her brain is trying to process. Our Queen is a submissive.

Garrett suspected as much from their encounters at The Fortress. She complied to his commands without hesitancy. Accepted his control of her body—when she'd cum, pushing her limits. He marveled at her grace in their power exchange.

Now, we can't wait to get Signy to Club Sol & Mani New York. Explore more of her sub side as her Doms and to introduce her to the BDSM lifestyle. It's one of six exclusive luxury members only BDSM clubs for wolf shifters. The location in South Beach is the flagship with the other five in the remaining territories. Each pack runs their club under the direction of Viggo since they're a part of the Larson Enterprises' properties division he heads.

Our club occupies a former bank in Manhattan's Financial District, close to Moen, Inc.'s headquarters. Sections focus on the distinct elements of the lifestyle. Exhibition where demonstrations and performance rooms provide entertainment—or inspiration. The Dungeon a spacious section devoted to public forms of BDSM play. Those not in the lifestyle may think it's a medieval dungeon for torture with the St. Andrew's Crosses, spanking benches, chains suspended from the ceiling, and more. To us, the pieces and assorted whips, floggers, canes, and implements are only to be expected. And enjoyed by all partners. For those who prefer privacy, they may reserve suites—each outfitted for its theme.

When Signy wondered about females in our beds, she needn't worry. We satisfied our carnal needs at the club. Soon she will join us.

Yesterday, we began her preparation for her first visit by exploring various apparatuses, implements, and toys delivered with the new bed—the *other items* Garrett mentioned. Her eyes glowed as we explained BDSM and the lifestyle we lead as Doms. She admitted she enjoys giving up control to us. It allows her mind freedom to just be in the moment and relish in her pleasure.

Her eagerness helped us decide to progress her based on her interests and tolerance. She surprised us with her willingness to go beyond her limits. As experienced Doms, we understand a sub's body and how far to go. She hasn't used her safeword yet.

And here we are in the new playroom.

Garrett warmed her up on the spanking bench, ending with a finger-fucked-induced orgasm that convulsed her entire body before we bound her to the cross. Dolph skillfully flogs her, amping the pleasure, as evidenced by the juices dripping down her thighs and puddling on the floor beneath her.

I capture another gasp and sigh, unable to separate myself from her delectable mouth. My fingertips skim down the centerline of her torso. Her muscles quiver beneath my caress. I wait for Dolph to strike, then pinch her clit. She wails as her hips buck. Her dripping pussy presses against my palm. I slip a finger inside and stroke her G-spot. Her inner walls quiver as she moans.

"Pain and pleasure, pet," I murmur against her kiss-swollen lips. "Lose yourself in it. Do you understand?"

Another slap, and she moans, "Yes, Sir."

Such a good girl.

My lips lift in a smile against her slack mouth.

Dolph

In between strikes of the flogger, I watch Colin kiss our sweet sub and whisper to her. When he drives his finger inside her pussy, I nearly cum in my jeans. Her honey cries—along with the intoxicating scent of the juices leaking from her pussy—fills the playroom, and my nostrils. I close my eyes and inhale deeply.

No female smells as intoxicating as our mate.

My heavy balls tighten. I squeeze the head of my dick to slow the need to fuck her right now. A couple more swings of the flogger, and she'll beg for more than Colin's finger.

After the last swing, I drop the flogger and prowl towards her. I press my front against her back. She winces when the rough cotton of my jeans touches her reddened ass. I kiss the back of her neck as my fingers massage the heated flesh.

"You did well, sub," I murmur against her damp skin. "Now it's time for your reward. Ready?"

She shudders as I grind my cock along the crack of her ass. The ass Garrett will claim first.

"Y—Yes, Sir," she exhales.

I crouch to release her ankles from the cuffs while Colin and Garrett remove the wrist cuffs. She collapses into my awaiting arms with a sigh. My cock punches the buttons on my jeans. With a quickness, I carry her to the giant bed and settle her on the white silk sheets. She hisses at the contact and stares up at me with hooded eyes. Her arms lift as her knees splay in welcome.

Fuck yes.

The metal buttons damn near pop off as I rip open my jeans. My cock tumbles free and smacks my abs. I shove the jeans down my hips and kick them off. Knees drop onto the bed. I lift her legs and brush open-mouthed kisses along the insides of her calves, up her thighs, and press my mouth to her sweet pussy. A long lick from one hole to the other has her legs trembling in my hands. She closes her eyes on a guttural moan.

It's all I need.

One hand cups her ass while the other lines the head of my cock to her dripping pussy. Both hands clutch her ass. My hips snap forward to impale her on my cock.

Her eyes snap wide as her jaw goes slack in a soundless

wail. Her perfect tits bounce from the impact as fingers grip my wrists.

"Oh! You're so *big*," she pants when words return. "Fuck!"

Her little pussy stretches to accommodate my girth and length. I bottom out, balls deep in her tight, slick heat. My heavy sac tingles. *Fuck* is right.

Drawing on all my control, I give her a moment to adjust. My hips swivel in a slow circle until her body relaxes. The blown pupils of her ice blue eyes meet my hooded topaz ones.

"Please fuck me, Sir."

I thought I'd blow her mind. She just flipped the script on me.

I growl and tighten my grip. Hips draw back and jerk forward, plunging my cock deep within her pussy. She screams and thrashes. Her pussy clenches, squeezing the life out of my dick.

"Cum as much as you want," I bite out between thrusts.

She raises her arms and claws the silk sheets above her head as it whips left and right. Flushed and glistening with sweat, she's a beauty to behold. Her cries like a symphony as I build her to a crescendo.

"Cum. One. More. Time. Now!"

I grunt as her pussy walls clamp on my cock. They flutter as her back bows with a scream of my name. A barbaric growl rips from my mouth as my cock swells and pulses. Hot ropes of cum jettison from the tip filling her pussy as it milks me for every drop.

My hips continue to move as I fuck her through another orgasm. I don't stop until she collapses to the bed, spent and sated. Gently, I slip my cock from her pussy. A crease forms between her eyebrows. But she doesn't utter a sound.

I watch my cum ooze from her swollen pussy lips. Something primal in me takes over. I push it back inside, not wanting a drop wasted. My pup will swell her belly. Her pussy accepts it greedily as her hole clenches. I drop a kiss on her engorged clit. Our combined release coats my lips. Reluctantly, I slip from between her thighs.

Garrett and Colin stand holding their flaccid dicks. Cum coats their fists and collects on the floor.

I smirk and head to the en suite bathroom. Returning to the bed, I clean her with a warm damp cloth, smooth tendrils of her damp ebony black hair off her face, and tuck her beneath the sheets. A last kiss pressed to her mouth, and I rise.

Transfixed, we stand at the foot of the bed and watch her curl onto her side. A contented sigh slips past her parted lips.

I don't know what they're thinking. But I know our fated mate has me under her spell. What I didn't expect was for her to adapt so quickly to the D/s lifestyle. Yet, she's the one in control as my body comes to life from her sweet innocence yet determination to impress us—the experienced ones.

If she enjoys this quickly put together playroom, she'll love Club Sol & Mani New York. And I can't wait to introduce her to it.

But first we must introduce her to the New York Wolves Pack as our fated mate and Luna.

SIGNY

"ARE YOU READY YET? Dinner starts in ten minutes."

"Almost! Five seconds!"

I scramble around my new mini boutique, flinging dresses, a jumpsuit, skirts, and blouses in my search for an appropriate outfit to meet the pack officially.

Aside from being mated to my males, Garrett as the Alpha makes me the Luna. It's an important role I'm more than familiar with because of my mother.

The Luna is the right hand to the Alpha. She helps him to govern the pack, particularly the she-wolves. She advises him and offers support. The better they work together, the more harmonious the pack. I know the pack will expect more from me as the daughter of a Luna well-respected throughout all territories.

So, it's not just the outfit. It's how I present myself. I

want our introduction to be perfect. Set the foundation for mutual trust and respect.

My gaze lands on a pair of black suede pants. They hug my curves and showcase my toned legs. I slip them on and pair them with a loose-fitting black silk blouse tucked in. A pair of black suede ankle boots complete the look. My hair cascades down my back to brush my ass. I twirl in the trifold mirror to study each angle. Strong and sexy.

I grab my mobile and hurry from the bedroom. At the top of the stairs, I pause to admire my males in the entry.

Garrett left his jet black hair loose hanging to his shoulder blades. It frames his sculpted cheekbones and freshly shave face. A blue cashmere sweater highlights his glacial eyes. A pair of navy wool trousers can't hide his muscular thighs. Long legs lead to boots. Power personified.

Light from the chandelier glints on the golden strands of Dolph's buzzed hair as he paces the stone floor, boots silent like a predator. The muscles in his long legs flex beneath black wool trousers. A black button-up shirt beneath a black vest rounds out his outfit. He's sleek and sexy.

My gaze shifts to Colin, who caught sight of me drooling above them. He stares with amber eyes darkened to burnished gold with desire. The corner of his lush mouth lifts in a sexy smirk surrounded by stubble on his jaw. The tip of his tongue glides along his lower lip before he drags it between his teeth. My pussy clenches, remembering all the places that same tongue drove me over the edge again and again an hour ago.

Entranced, I barely notice the black v-neck sweater and the black leather pants stuffed into heavy boots. The bad boy all the way. And I love it.

"Oh, there you are," Dolph says, as he comes to a stop and stares up at me.

Garrett's gaze lifts, and his eyes flash as they travel over my body. They pause at every curve. The heat in his stare puckers my nipples, sure to be evident against the silk. He smirks as he strides to the foot of the stairs and raises his hand for me.

Deliberately, I sway my hips as I slowly descend. Our bond pulses as their desire increases. By the hooded eyes that devour my every move, I can tell they feel my mutual desire. Garrett sweeps me into his arms and kisses me with the passion of his yearning. I groan and respond in kind, fingers tangling in his hair.

"Okay. As much as I'm in favor of taking this action upstairs, we need to go," Dolph says and opens the door.

A cool breeze blows in. Colin holds my new parka while I slip into it. Naturally, they go without outwear. He takes my hand and leads me to the SUV where Dolph sits at the wheel. We climb inside and drive to the dining hall.

Tingles of nervousness skitter through me.

Garrett shifts in the passenger seat and pins me with an intense stare.

"Do not worry, Signy. You are the perfect Luna for our pack—smart, strong, gracious."

My heart warms as Dolph and Colin agree. I squeeze Colin's hand and thank them.

As we enter the dining hall, the laughter and conversation quiet down until it's silent. Every head turns to the four of us. My butterflies flutter in my chest.

Garrett—who already holds my hand—glances about the room and strides down the center aisle towards the head table. I keep pace with him, a smile on my face as I nod at the pack members we pass. Garrett holds out my chair, and I sit, folding my napkin over my lap.

I glance around the table. My smile widens at the sight of Estrid. I jump from my chair and rush to embrace her. Tears prick the backs of my eyes as I'm reminded of the monsters Blaise and Bernard.

"Hello, child. I'm so happy you returned!"

"Me too. And seeing you so radiant makes me even happier."

I give her another squeeze and return to my seat. Garrett helps me to sit again with Colin beside me and Dolph on the other side of Garrett. He introduces me to their parents at the table with us, then rises.

"New York Wolves Pack, as you probably heard from the wolf vine"—he pauses as the room fills with laughter —"The gods blessed Dolph, Colin, and me with a fated mate. Although the circumstances of meeting her were unfortunate for some of her pack mates, we are thankful to have her."

He extends his hand to me, and I take it to stand beside him.

"Signy Larson, daughter of Marcus and Sigrid Larson, former Alpha and Luna of the Miami Wolves Pack, sister to Jagger Larson the current Alpha and to Viggo Larson. Meet your new Luna!"

The pack members clap and wolf whistle, stomping their feet. The dining hall rocks with their enthusiasm.

Garrett pulls me flush to his body and kisses me senseless. Not to be outdone, Colin spins me to him and fuses his lips to mine. I'm breathless by the time Dolph grabs me and slants his mouth over my slack one. Dazed and elated, I return their fervent kisses.

The rest of the dinner passes with members stopping by the table to introduce themselves and to welcome me to the pack. They ask me how I'm recovering and offer their support. Many of the females invite me for lunch. Garrett's mother Idonea offers to mentor me as Luna. I accept gladly.

My mates keep constant watch. Garrett and Colin's hands rest on my thighs possessively, even while they speak to others. Dolph frequently leaves his chair to rub my shoulders or to kiss the top of my head. I'm surrounded by their love. We're together at last.

And I couldn't be happier.

 *arrett*

"W HAT'S SO urgent we had to cancel our meetings and fly back from the city?"

Thyra glances over her shoulder at Dolph, Colin, and me as we enter her office on Moen Island. She called twenty minutes ago but wouldn't disclose any information until we arrived. She points at a monitor.

"I set up alerts on the Dark Web to track chatter about breeding rings, auctions, pups—you get the gist," she responds and swirls her finger to encompass the four monitors.

I peer closer but can't decipher the meanings of the conversations that fill the screens.

"They're in a code I just cracked. The fuckers used a system—"

"We don't need the details," I interrupt. "What does it mean?"

She nods.

"Since you guys eliminated Blaise and Bernard's ring, a new one cropped up. It was second to theirs as the most active. It's based on the outskirts of the Aspen Wolves' territory, close to our border with them. This ring took over the contacts the other one had. And now, there's chatter about a big shipment and subsequent auction."

"Fuck!"

"Where and when?"

"Those bastards!"

Thyra shakes her head, eyes flashing, a curl to her lip.

"It gets worse. They brag about capturing daughters and a sister of Alphas, the new sought-after targets. Seems like Blaise raised the bar by having Signy. The starting bids are $1 million, each. The auction starts tomorrow night."

I hiss in a breath as my hand grips the back of my neck.

The fucking gall!

We knew more rings existed—we've fought enough of them. But we didn't expect them to jump back into operation so soon after Blaise and Bernard lost control. Obviously, the others used their loss to increase their reach.

Well, too damn bad. We'll end them the same as we

have others. We won't stop until we finish every single one of them. They will no longer terrorize she-wolves and human females. Not under our watch.

The short notice means we need to act now. We gather as much intel from Thyra as possible. She'll update us while we're on the move. We leave her office and go to mine, where I call the Ruling Council.

Leif tells us his sister didn't return home last night. He vows to kill. The Las Vegas and the Sedona Alphas inform us of missing daughters. All are in an uproar.

We spend the next hour strategizing. Each pack will converge on the area for what will be a major battle, if not the war. At least I hope we can end all breeding rings with this mission. It's a fight we've done long enough. Thyra says a few rings combined. So perhaps we'll have our chance to destroy them in one swoop. We end the call.

Dolph runs a hand over his buzzed hair. His eyebrows pinch over concerned tawny eyes.

"We're ready for this. But Signy is going to be upset."

Colin groans and slumps against his chair.

So engrossed in the situation, I forgot about our mate and what this means to her. Damn, how can I ever forget her? Dolph is right.

I scrub a hand over my face.

We ended our seclusion the night of Signy's introductory dinner. That was a week ago. We're just getting into our daily routine. Signy converted an extra room on our mansion's first floor into an office. She goes to work every morning. Well, after we fuck her thoroughly. A reminder of her mates before we take the helicopter to Moen, Inc. At night, we eat dinner and recall our days. Sometimes we watch a movie or go to the playroom—what's quickly become her favorite place in our residence. Then we climb into our massive bed. A normal life.

But Dolph, Colin, and I are nowhere near normal. We run a multibillion-dollar arms and aircraft manufacturing company and lead dangerous missions on the side. We're not the average Joes. That was fine before we mated. Now, we have Signy and her feelings to consider.

"Yeah. And it couldn't happen at a worse time," I agree with a shake of my head. "But we made a pledge to rid the territories of these breeder rings, and we will follow through."

Colin flattens his lips but nods.

"We better tell her now since we leave soon," Dolph says and stands.

Colin and I follow him from the office.

My heart lies heavy in my chest.

I pray to the gods Signy will understand and even more so, we return to her. My heart clenches. I rub a fist over my chest. This is exactly why I hesitated to claim her. Now, the deed is done, and we face the consequences.

SIGNY

. . .

"I CANNOT BELIEVE you only told Sage! I get she's our Luna. But I'm as much of a clothes wolf as you!"

I giggle as Wren—my sister-in-law via Tag—pouts. Her mink brown eyes narrow at me.

"That's so unfair. Besides, I'd love to help you source pieces," she continues, then claps her hands bouncing on her chair. Her rich mahogany brown hair bounces along with her. "We must throw a launch party for you! Oh! Better yet, do one in each territory since Signy's Secret Cache is online and accessible the globe over. Do you think the European wolf shifters will allow us to host parties in Paris, London, and Milan?"

I grin at the monitor as she rambles on.

Her excitement matches my own.

Since Garrett gave me free rein, I converted a room in our residence to my office. I decorated it in shades of pale pinks and creams with platinum accents. Antique French furniture fills the sun-drenched space—a large writing desk and chair, twin sofas, coffee and end tables, bookshelves, and light fixtures with an Aubusson rug over the bleached hardwood floor. The room evokes a sumptuous boudoir.

"I'm sure the Alphas will give their approval if we ask nicely," I tease.

She rolls her eyes.

"Well, events are my thing. So, I'll handle them for you. Now, tell me more."

An hour later, I sit back in my chair and spin to face the French doors. More signs of spring appear as tiny buds dot the bushes outside. The ground is clear of snow. Even though it's still a dull green, patches of more vibrant blades emerge. A blue jay lands on a branch. Its feathers remind me of Garrett's gorgeous eyes. Spring brings a fresh start, a time for rebirth.

I sigh with happiness.

A knock at the door draws me back to the office. A maid appears with a tray of tea and cookies—my new afternoon treats. She sets it on the coffee table between the sofas. I thank her and settle in with the latest copy of *Vogue* magazine.

An unexpected chill runs through me. My hand trembles as I replace the teacup on the saucer. I glance around the office for the source of the cold air. The windows remain closed, and the door shut. Odd. I cross my arms over my chest and rub my palms along them.

My heart leaps into my throat at a second knock on my door. It opens, and Garrett, Dolph, and Colin file in. One look at the strained expressions on their faces, and I know the source of the sudden chill. My throat works as I attempt to speak. Instead, I gesture at the sofas. They sit—Garrett beside me and Dolph and Colin opposite. I shift to face Garrett. Alarm bells blare in my head.

"We learned of a larger breeding ri—"

"No!"

I jump to my feet, shaking my head vigorously. But Garrett catches my wrist and tugs me onto his lap. I slap at his shoulders, still shaking my head. Tears spring to my eyes. I cannot—I *will* not—lose my mates. Not now. Not ever.

"Baby… Baby… Listen to me. You won't lose us," Garrett says as he grips my wrists in one hand and swipes tears from my eyes with the other fingers.

I didn't realize I spoke aloud, or the tears tracked down my cheeks.

"P—Please, Garrett… Please don't go. Don't leave me. You promised we'd be together always."

Pain flashes across his face. He opens his mouth, but no words come out.

"Signy," Dolph says as he strokes my back. "We're not breaking our promise. This is a mission we must complete. You, most of all, know what's at stake for those females. Please understand."

Colin kneels beside me and catches my wobbly chin between his thumb and index finger. He turns my face to align our eyes. His shine golden.

"Signy, we love you more than you can ever know. That love binds us and will always bring us back to you."

He slants his mouth over mine. He kisses me until the shock leaves me. I kiss him back with all the passion and love I possess for them. He growls and deepens the kiss.

Hands and claws rip my clothes from my body. I'm laid

out on the Aubusson rug, where they prove how much they love me as they promise to return. Even as they love on me, I can't help the ache gnawing at my heart.

Gods, please return them to me. *Please.*

A few hours later, I stand in wolf form on the bluff, eyes on the helicopter carrying my three fated mates away from me and our home on Moen Island.

After you claimed me, you promised we'd be together forever. Now, you leave me to battle monsters who can ruin our happily ever after.

I throw my head back and howl at the inky night sky.

olin

"THE LAYOUT MATCHES the images provided by Thyra. It's their typical setup, with a building for the auction surrounded by trucks with the females and pups. The only differences are the additional vehicles, presumably from the bidders. We go in as planned. Kill all members of the ring but the leaders. Detain the bidders with the silver handcuffs and ankle shackles. We will transport them to the Aspen pack's lodge. Understood?"

Agreement of Garrett's command carries through our earpieces as we amass around the location. Dolph and I nod as he stares at us with determination. He shut down the guilty expression he wore since we left Signy crying at the mansion.

After we made love to her, she reined in her emotions while we showered and dressed. Even as she told us she'll see us soon, she maintained her poise. But as we walked towards the SUV, we heard her sorrowful wail. Our bond thrummed with her pain. It still does.

I rub my knuckles against my chest, covered by a combat vest.

Silently, we approach the location, using the surrounding trees as cover. The moonless night sky aids us in blending with the shadows. Wolves pad along beside us as we converge in both forms onto the property. The air crackles with electricity. I sniff the air but only scent a large amount of wolf shifters, indistinguishable from the breeding ring. No worries. We tied black bandanas around our necks to differentiate us from those fuckers.

I check the knot on mine. I promised Signy I'd come back in one piece. She'd be pissed at me if my knot loosened, and I was mistaken for the enemy. My lips quirk at the thought of her railing on me once I healed. At least we'd have incredible makeup sex.

"Eagle in position."

"Owl in position."

"Hawk in position."

The list goes on until each of the six pack Alphas confirm they're ready. After Garrett gives the word, we move stealthily. The three of us—with our unit—move towards the building. The sounds of a few scuffles indicate they made contact with the breeding ring members. But we focus on securing the leaders we believe are in the building, as Blaise and Bernard were in Maine.

Two males flank the double doors of the abandoned barn. Garrett takes point with Dolph next. I follow with the others fanned out around me. We listen for sounds of activity. Low voices inside reach our ears. Garrett nods. The two at the doors slide them open.

A few lanterns towards the rear cast light. The voices drone on, unaware of our presence. No movement. The words repeat. Odd.

My gut churns as instinct flares.

Garrett steps forward.

A soft click reaches my ears. Followed by another and another still. A chain reaction.

I turn just as a sharp whistle whips through the air. A blast of heat and metal from behind knocks me face forward to the straw-covered floor. Males scream in agony. The scent of charred flesh mixes with the distinct almond smell from the dense putty-like material of blocks, lumps or sticks used in explosives. My weapons training mind picks up on the details, even as it registers the string of explosives in the barn.

Signy is going to be beyond pissed.

～

SIGNY

"No! No! No!"

I awake to the stench of burning flesh as blasts boom in my ears. I cover them, screaming as the threads to my mates spasm. My heart twists. The pain unbearable. Stars dance behind my closed eyelids. My breath stutters.

"Garrett… Dolph… Colin…"

I whisper the names of my fated mates.

Then darkness descends.

THANK you for reading *Signy Claimed*!

Their story concludes in *Signy Forever: A Wolf Shifter Fated Mates Reverse Harem Romance*. If you enjoyed this book, I would so appreciate your review as they make a huge difference for indie authors. Be sure to sign up for my newsletter for latest info about the series, new releases, and a FREE book **bit.ly/CLBooksDylanThe Rogue** for Dylan and Sasha's story! Turn the page for a preview of the start to the Billionaire Wolves Series— *Jagger The Temptation: A Wolf Shifter Fated Mates Paranormal Romance*.

PREVIEW JAGGER THE TEMPTATION: A WOLF SHIFTER FATED MATES PARANORMAL ROMANCE

agger

"The quarterly numbers show an increase in profits. More than projected because of the opening of the beach-front resort in Charleston earlier than planned. The general manager reports the property sold out for the first four months..."

I nod as my Vice President of Hotels and Resorts for Larson Enterprises, Inc. continues his update. My mind focuses partially on his presentation.

For the last few weeks, I can't seem to focus. I don't know whether lack of sleep causes the lapse or something else. Dreams of another dominate my nights. They remain just out of reach, on the fringes. But it's their silent pleas for help that keep me tossing. A vibration from them of fear and sadness draws me closer. My instinct kicks in, and I want to save them, protect them.

Each dream brings me closer to them. But they remain just out of reach. I wake tangled in silk sheets. An arm extended as my hand reaches for them. Last night I called a name. However, as the last vestiges of the dream slipped away, the name dissolved with it.

I growl low in my chest in frustration.

My COO shifts his gaze to me. His wolf senses picked up my displeasure with ease.

I shake my head at Tag Dahl.

He cocks his head at me.

As my best friend, he's known me since we were pups. Born within a few weeks of each other—him to our pack's enforcer and me to our Alpha—Tag knows me as well as I know myself. I haven't mentioned my dreams to him, not that he'd think me nuts. No. I just don't know what they mean and if they warrant a conversation for analysis.

And Tag would delve into their meaning.

As my beta, he's my right-hand man. Anything that involves me and can impact our pack, he wants to solve the puzzle.

But this one will remain under wraps until I figure it out. So, I shake my head again and turn my attention back to the presentation. Even as I will my mind to pay full attention. I remove my personal hat. Then I firmly affix the one for my roles as CEO and Chairman of the Board of the luxury hotels, fine dining, clubs, and lounges company my family founded in Miami.

An hour later, a persistent Tag strides along with me to my suite of offices in The Larson Tower on Biscayne Bay. We pass through the executive floor as staff—wolf shifter and human—acknowledge us. The unaware humans often stare in awe at our formidable sizes. We're both six feet, seven inches of pure muscle and move with predatory grace. We nod in return but continue without pause.

I know Tag wants to find out what's up with me. I'll allow his henpecking since we're so close. Otherwise, I do not tolerate others in my business. No. One.

"Alpha, you have a few voicemails, sir."

"Thanks, Ginny," I respond to my administrative assistant as I open the double doors of my office. "Kindly hold my calls."

"What's up, Jagger?"

I bite back an irritated growl—lack of sleep will have you pissed, even at your best friend who only wants to help.

"You want a drink?" I ask as I unbutton the jacket of my bespoke three-piece Brioni suit and stride to the bar cart. It's after five-thirty, and I can use a stiff one before I head out to Club Sol & Mani for some much-needed sexual relief.

"Sure, thanks."

I take my time pouring two fingers of scotch into the Baccarat crystal tumblers. Absolutely no rush to have Tag pick at my psyche. My ears pick up his almost silent huff, and I chuckle to myself.

"Don't delay this conversation, Jag. You've been off for a few weeks now, and I've given you space," he says, then nods his thanks for the liquor. "What's up with you?"

Again, I allow him to question me, even though I'm his Alpha and my word is final.

I lower myself onto the dove gray tufted leather sofa in the seating area. Tag takes a chair opposite and places an ankle over a knee. I sip my drink as I consider my words. He knows better than to interrupt at this point.

"Dreams."

He cocks his head at the simple one-worded response. I shrug and take another sip.

"For the past few weeks, dreams invade my sleep. Every. Single. Night. Someone's in trouble. But I can't catch their name or where they are to help them," I sigh and stare out the window.

The panoramic view across Biscayne Bay with jet skiers and megayachts on its dazzling surface out to the azure Atlantic Ocean helps to quiet the inner turmoil my wolf and I sense. He turns his massive silvery white head to stare at me with accusatory ice blue eyes. It's as though he knows something I don't and pissed I'm not aware. I run my fingers through my white blond hair as I think on it, then shake my head. No clue.

"What do you recall?" Tag asks as he leans forward and

places his elbows on his knees, the scotch tumbler balanced between his sizable hands.

I shrug.

"A brightness in the background prevents a clear view. I know it's outdoors since I hear the hum of insects and feel the warm sun on my skin. Naked skin. So, I must have shifted and returned to my human form."

Another sip of scotch, and I stand to pace my office.

Instinct tells me these are no ordinary dreams. But each morning I account for the whereabouts of my pack, and no one turns up missing. Not knowing who calls for my help drives me and my wolf mad.

I growl and toss back the rest of my scotch. A few long strides and I refill the tumbler.

"No one in our pack seems in trouble. I'll stop by the she-wolves' residences on my way home just to make sure. A few of our unmated males flew to New Orleans for the weekend. I'll shoot a text to them and make sure they didn't get into anything on Bourbon Street."

With a nod of agreement, I hold the decanter up. Tag declines a refill—ever the responsible one. Fine. It's not like wolf shifters can get drunk. Well, not too much. Our systems process substances differently from humans. All the better for us, especially when I'm in this pissy mood.

"Well, you know they say fated mates can have dreams about the other. The more frequent and intense they become, the closer the pair gets to their first encounter," Tag says. His emerald green eyes scan my face for a reaction. He knows I've waited all these years for my fated mate—and will continue to do so.

Despite my father's damn near daily persistence, I issue the claiming bite and complete the mating bond with a single she-wolf. The last eleven years of nearly nonstop mating runs, with the she-wolves in my pack and those from nearby cities—hell, even overseas. Or galas at our hotels and mixers at our clubs, an accidental encounter, all to persuade me to select a she-wolf as my mate. None of them tempt me in the slightest.

All the she-wolves desire to bond with me. Then the supposed prince—and they were eager to lose their slippers and thongs for me to pick up——now the Alpha of the Miami Wolves Pack. Correction, *Billionaire Wolves of Miami* as the other packs refer to us. With good reason, since we're the most powerful pack in the South.

Several millennia ago, Scandinavian Viking wolf shifters sailed from the Old World and landed along the East Coast of what's now the United States. The six packs headed by best friends who sought new lands moved throughout the continent to form territories with ours settling here. We maintain close ties with our brethren through friendship, mating, and business. Plus, our Ruling Council gatherings keep us informed of happenings throughout the packs.

And even going that far and wide, I have yet to meet my fated mate. However, I will wait for her.

Hell, my wolf demands it as he gets agitated when he

senses a she-wolf's burgeoning interest. Sure, he'll sit back while I fuck since it fills a need and doesn't equate to being mated. Wolf shifters—male and female—have strong sexual appetites. We don't have the same hang-ups as humans over casual sex, no sex before marriage, and whatever other bullshit they come up with. It's a part of our lives, just like eating or breathing. A need we won't suppress. Particularly with the built-up tension raging through my body. However, his pacing and snarls have increased recently, too.

So maybe Tag is on to something.

My *fated* mate.

A she-wolf whose scent I was born with teasing my nostrils. When she appears, I will recognize her by her distinct scent. No other will bear her uniqueness. Someday we will meet. I will give her my claiming bite, and we will have our mate bonding ceremony for all the clans to witness. I will make her mine forever.

The thought she may be in trouble makes my blood boil and my wolf snap his teeth, ears flat to his head. Our protective instinct on high alert.

So, I won't give up on finding my fated mate—or on us. No matter how many times my father bugs me about the need to bond with another. I'm no longer the teen who had to obey.

I am Alpha now.

~

"WE'RE HERE, ALPHA."

I glance up from my mobile screen and out the tinted window.

So focused on business emails, I didn't notice my driver pull my Black Badge Rolls-Royce Cullinan into the driveway for Club Sol & Mani Miami. The flagship of six exclusive, luxury, members only BDSM clubs Larson Enterprises owns sits on Ocean Drive directly across from the Atlantic Ocean in a South Beach historic, beachfront gated mansion.

"Great, thank you, Cole," I respond. "I'll take it from here and will text when I'm ready to go home."

"Yes, Alpha. I'll get the door for you."

I wave him off and reach for the handle, only for the club's valet to open the door. A nod to Cole and a thanks in the form of a hundred to the young wolf shifter, and I stride to the scrolled wrought-iron and glass doors of the Spanish-style mansion. Laughter from members as they frolic in the mosaic-tiled pool within the sun-filled courtyard floats in the balmy evening air.

"Good evening, Alpha," the doorman says with a respectful bow of his head. I shake his hand and palm off another hundred. He thanks me as I move on.

"Hello, Alpha!" The two she-wolf greeters chorus cheerfully as I walk through the opulent lobby to the elevators. Another two C-notes and I'm on the elevator headed to my personal suite.

Tonight, I'll play in privacy rather than amongst other

members in Exhibition where demonstrations and performance rooms provide entertainment—or inspiration. Nor will the Dungeon do, despite my affinity for the spacious section devoted to public forms of BDSM play. Those not in the lifestyle may think it's a medieval dungeon for torture with the St. Andrew's Crosses, spanking benches, chains suspended from the ceiling, and more. To me, the pieces and assorted whips, floggers, canes, and implements are only to be expected.

The soft thrum of sensual music greets me as I step out of the elevator and into the hallway. The rhythm vibrates through my core as intended to amp arousal for what lies behind the closed doors of the eight private suites. Members can reserve them in advance should they prefer the same privacy I wish for tonight.

Each suite decorated by theme has various BDSM pieces, implements, and toys. A nice variety of options to choose from. However, my suite remains for my personal use only.

I press my palm against the plate by the door of the corner suite, and the locks disengage.

"Good evening, Alpha."

My head jerks up. What the fuck?! I allow no one in my space without my consent. My ice blue eyes adjust to the candlelit room. On my custom-built mahogany wood, king-size bed cornered by four thick carved posters and a brass lattice canopy with rings strategically attached sits a she-wolf from my pack. And not just any she-wolf. The sable-haired hellion.

"Melissa, what the fuck are you doing in my suite?!" I snarl as I stalk towards her.

She jerks back as though slapped but recovers quickly. Fully naked, she rises from the bed with the prowess of a wolf in hunt mode and slinks towards me. Amber eyes glow in the candlelight. She tosses her waist-length sable brown hair over her shoulders. Her sleek figure with high perky tits tipped by puckered rosy nipples, flat belly, narrow waist, slim hips, and long, toned legs would make any male salivate.

Not me.

Even though I planned to fuck her tonight—after I *invited* her to my suite—my stomach churns at the thought as my wolf growls low in his broad chest. He's not happy, nor am I.

Melissa is one of my regular sexual partners. We scratch the itch for each other from time to time. However, it's not like we're exclusive. Many a she-wolf join me for carnal pleasures. As Melissa has with other males. And I've made it clear I am not interested in bonding with her.

But after this stunt, this may very well be the last time I hookup with her. If she thinks she can enter my domain uninvited, she's confused. And I will speak with the club manager about her gaining unapproved access.

I have no intention of giving Melissa any ideas.

Not happening.

For one, Melissa thinks she's the alpha since the other male wolf shifters in our pack bow down to her beauty and succumb to her whims. I won't have it.

Not to mention she's a bully. Another trait I will not tolerate. I treat everyone in our pack with respect. They may not be my equal, but I don't make them feel less than.

And the most important reason… She's not my fated mate. The only wolf shifter who will enter my domain as she pleases.

My wolf agrees with a flick of his feathery tail.

"Melissa, I have told you we fuck. Nothing more"—I raise my hand to stop her response—"You have no right to enter my personal suite without my permission. None. Get dressed. I will inform the club manager not to allow you entry ever again. This is it. Do you understand?"

She blinks, then her mouth opens.

I fold my arms over my chest and stand with feet spread far apart in a dominant manner as I pin her with an arctic gaze.

Naturally, Melissa glares back and mimics my stance as her eyes blaze golden fire.

"Jag—"

"Alpha! Alpha, Melissa. And do not forget it. We may have fucked. But you will respect me as your Alpha. Get. Dressed. And. Go. Now."

She lifts her chin in defiance, then reconsiders when I slap my sizable palm on my muscular thigh. Her eyes widen at the warning. Then she scurries to the chair and gathers her clothes to her flushed chest.

"Yes, Alpha!" She exclaims.

With a stern eye, I watch as she dresses quickly.

Melissa stops at the door and glances at me over her shoulder. Her oval-shaped face pinched with worry. She knows she took it too far this time.

"Sorry, Alpha," she whispers, then opens the door and leaves.

I sigh and sink onto the bed.

Well, there goes the idea of releasing tension. More just built up.

With his tongue hanging out from the side of his mouth, my wolf yips. Ice blue eyes gleam with mirth. It's as though he laughs at my misfortune.

I growl at him and slump back on the navy blue silk pillows. My thoughts drift to my conversation with Tag. Perhaps fate doesn't want me with another since my mate will appear soon. My eyes close on a sigh.

Where are you?

Click the Image Below or Visit books2read.com/u/ mZEL2e For Your Copy

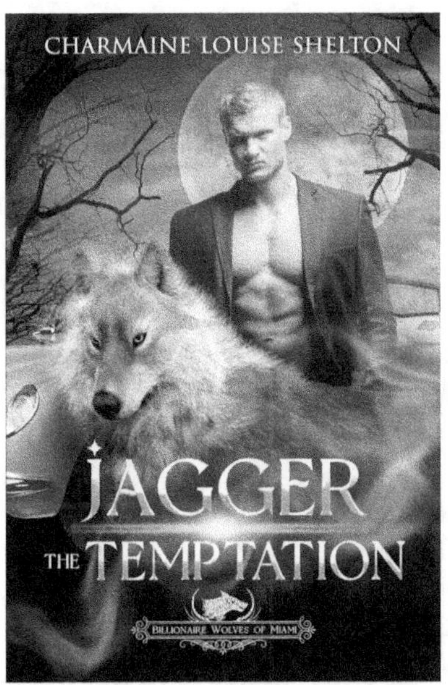

Jagger The Temptation: A Wolf Shifter Fated Mates
Paranormal Romance

NEXT IN SERIES SIGNY
FOREVER: A WOLF SHIFTER
FATED MATES REVERSE HAREM
ROMANCE

My wolf shifter fated mates claimed me. But will we make it to our happily ever after, and will it last forever?

Garrett the grumpy leader whose glacial eyes pierce my soul.

Dolph the comforting beta whose musky masculine scent makes me shiver.

Colin the brute enforcer whose snark is as good as his bite.

I'M their fated mate and their Queen of the New York Wolves Pack.

· · ·

THEIR SPICY REVERSE harem paranormal romance is a standalone trilogy in the sizzling Billionaire Wolves Series of interconnecting stories featuring wolf shifter fated mates romance. Get a glimpse of their dynamism in other books.

Click the Image Below or Visit books2read.com/u/ 3LNQND For Your Copy

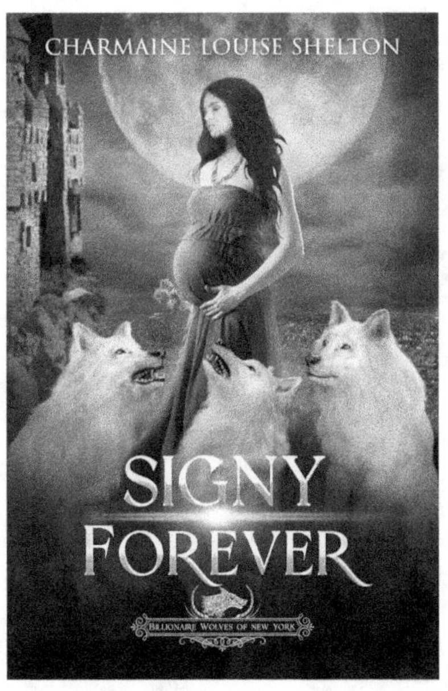

Signy Forever: A Wolf Shifter Fated Mates Reverse
Harem Romance

WANT FREE BOOKS?

Want to know what happened to Jagger's best friend Dylan? Find out in *Dylan The Rogue: A Wolf Shifter Fated Mates Paranormal Romance* your FREE Book!

Click Cover Below or visit **bit.ly/ CLBooksDylanTheRogue** to subscribe to my newsletter for latest news and launches, books from my author friends, and sizzling reads in book promotions. Plus, start reading the steamy fated mates romance for bad boy wolf shifter Dylan.

To read her current works, visit her Ream Stories account bit.ly/CharmaineLouiseBooksCoterie.

ABOUT CHARMAINE LOUISE SHELTON

Charmaine Louise Shelton loves a dominant Alpha hero—human, shifter, or vampire—as long as he's a billionaire and sexy as sin! Her romance novels take readers into the heroes' glitzy, glamorous, steamy worlds as they chase after independent women who unexpectedly capture their hearts. Want to experience some more? Download a free book at CharmaineLouiseBooks.com! To read her current works, visit her Ream Stories account bit.ly/Charmaine LouiseBooksCoterie.

Find her at:
CharmaineLouiseBooks.com

Follow her on social media on your favorite channels below and **download your Free Book** at Charmaine LouiseBooks.com.

Fulfill Your Desires.

bookbub.com/authors/charmaine-louise-shelton
tiktok.com/@charmainelouisebooks
youtube.com/@charmainelouisebooks
facebook.com/CharmaineLouiseBooks
instagram.com/charmainelouisebooks
goodreads.com/charmainelouisebooks

<u>A Trilogy of Desires Sebastian & Lola Parts I-III</u>

<u>A Trilogy of Desires Roger & Leonie Parts I-III</u>

<u>A Trilogy of Desires Malcolm & Starr Parts I-III</u>

<u>Series Extras</u>

<u>Series Playlist</u>

STEELE INTERNATIONAL, INC. - JACKSON CORPORATION

A BILLIONAIRES ROMANCE SERIES CROSSOVER

<u>Tempt My Desires Lachlan & Haley Part I</u>

<u>Tease My Desires Lachlan & Haley Part I</u>

<u>Grant My Desires Lachlan & Haley Part III</u>

<u>Intrigue My Desires Harris & Kat Part I</u>

<u>Decode My Desires Harris & Kat Part II</u>

<u>Honor My Desires Harris & Kat Patt III</u>

<u>A Trilogy of Desires Lachlan & Haley Parts I-III</u>

<u>A Trilogy of Desires Harris & Kat Parts I-III</u>

<u>Series Extras</u>

<u>Series Playlist</u>

JACKSON CORPORATION

A BILLIONAIRES ROMANCE SERIES

Evoke My Desires Laurent & Yessenia Prequel

Light My Desires Laurent & Yessenia Part I

BILLIONAIRE WOLVES SERIES

WOLF SHIFTER FATED MATES PARANORMAL ROMANCE

MIAMI

Jagger The Awakening

(Available in Billionaire Wolves of Miami —The Complete
Collection)

<u>Dylan The Rogue</u>

(Available Exclusively to Subscribers)

<u>Jagger The Temptation</u>

<u>Rust The Rejected</u>

<u>Tag The Redemption</u>

DEDICATION

To my awesome and dedicated beta readers and ARC Team, my amazing author friends, and this incredible community for their support.

And most of all to you, my loyal readers who love these couples as much as I do.

Thank you!

Fulfill Your Desires.

xoxo
Charmaine Louise Shelton